THE
COIN

Nathan Jones

Introduction

This story and the characters are purely fictional. But I can't leave out that maybe in certain real life situations, it's certainly possible for a situation like in this story and the characters can be a real life event. So kick back, relax and enjoy your reading.

Yours Truly,

Nathaniel I. Jones, Jr.

Acknowledgements:

,
The acknowledgements first and foremost is my belief and life of knowing, THE LORD GOD THROUGH HIS SON JESUS CHRIST, from a very early age. This is how I was raised by my parents. Nathaniel I. Jones, Sr. and Catherine Naomi Jones, my Father and Mother. They both are in Heaven, with THE LORD GOD now. I have always had a knack for writing at an early age. I've had a lot of life challenges throughout my life, ups and downs and all arounds. But I Thank, THE LORD GOD THROUGH HIS SON JESUS CHRIST for keeping me safe and strong through the times, to come to a point in my life where I can really express myself through my writings.

TO SHARI

PEACE AND LOVE

Nathan

2-23-2016

Chapter 1

In the summer of 2010 in the city of Santa Monica, California there was a young man named Jake, who was born and raised in New Orleans, LA. He left home when he was about 23 years old to come out to California to pursue a music or acting career.

He was residing in an apartment on 9th street between Arizona and Broadway in Santa Monica, California. He had a waiter job at The Main Lobster House Restaurant. His place of employment was ten blocks from where he lived and he would catch the bus to and from there every day he had to work.

One day Jake was going to work and he stopped at the coffee shop on the corner from where he lived to get change in order to catch the bus. On and off he would do that, but this particular day the cashier at the coffee shop gave him his change and in the change there was a quarter that was bent on all sides.

Jake looked at it and started to give it back, but while he was looking at it, the coin started to tremble around in his hand with the other coins. He didn't say anything about it to other people, who was standing around in the coffee shop. He just folded his hand with coins in it and walked out headed towards the bus stop.

When he reached the bus stop, he sat on the bus bench waiting for the bus and he opened his hand to look at his change to get bus fare out and took another look at the bent quarter. When he opened his hand, the bent quarter started to jump up and down in his hand. He was kind of afraid, but for some strange reason he got curious and said what the hell. He took the bent quarter and the rest of the change, minus the bus fare, he put the change back in his pocket and at that time his mind was wondering how and why this bent quarter was moving about in his hand. It wasn't moving around in his pocket.

While sitting on the bus bench, waiting for the bus, Jake started to have weird thoughts to see all things in a different perspective. He would see a man in the passenger seat of a car stopped at a red light looking mean at him (at Jake). Meanwhile Jake was evaluating which ways he can kill him and dismantle his body and dispose of it. But his real self wasn't realizing he's having these peculiar thoughts and ideas. The bus arrived, he got on and said to the bus driver:

Jake! Hello, how are you?

Bus driver: OK, Thank you and yourself?

Jake: I'm good, Thank you.

He took a seat on the bus, rode to his stop, got off and walked across the street to his work, walked inside the back door of the restaurant, and punched in with his timecard.

Fellow co-worker (Tom): Hey what's going on Jake?

Tom was standing in the hallway leading to the dressing room.

Jake: Everything's alright. How are you, Tom?

Tom: I'm good, ready for this day?

Jake: Ready, as I can be.

Meanwhile! He would off and on be thinking in the back of his mind, why was that quarter jumping up and down in his hand. Jake went into the dressing room, put his stuff in his locker and put on his apron and went to work. He walked into the restaurant and started waiting on the customers.

All the customers he waited on were pleasant except for one guy who was drunk.

Jake: Would you like to order, Sir?

Customer: What do you think! Sure I would like to order.

Jake kept his cool and said what would you like to have?
The guy looked at the menu!
The customer ordered the Number #10 on the menu with black coffee.
Jake took his order and on returning with his order, he approached the customer and said:

Jake: Here is your order, Sir, #10 with black coffee.

The #10 was waffles and pork sausage patties.

Customer: Paused, looked at the food and said, what in the fuck is this? I didn't order this shit.

Jake: Aaaahhh, forgive me Sir. But in reality Jake was so pissed and angry at this guy he could have grabbed one of those utensils sitting on the table and stabbed that dude in the chest. But instead he said to the customer:

Jake: Excuse me Sir, let me go get the manager.

Customer: Yea! You better get somebody. Cause I ain't eating this shit.

Jake retrieved the manager and they both walked over to the table where the customer was.

Manager: Is there a problem, Sir?

Customer: Yea there is. I didn't order this shit.

Manager: Aaahhh, excuse me Sir we can't have that kind of language in our establishment.

Customer: So what the fuck, I don't have to eat in here anyway, fuck you!

 The customer got up and walked out of the restaurant.

Manager talking to Jake:

Manager: How did all that get started?

Jake: He came in drunk with a chip on his shoulder (a grudge). I was patient with him but it was of no use. That's why I came and got you.

Manager: OK good, you did the right thing, we won't call the police this time. He's gone! If he comes back we won't let him in and if he gives us any problems then we'll have him arrested.

Jake: OK, Thanks Sir.

Manager: You are welcome. Are you okay?

Jake: Yes, I'm good.

Manager: Are you good to finish your shift?

Jake: Yes, I'm good.

Manager: OK, let me get back to what I was doing. I'll talk to you later.

Jake: OK Sir, Thanks.

Manager: You're welcome.

Manager walked off and went back into his office.

Jake resumed back to work.
 Jake worked the rest of his shift, went and punched out and left the restaurant on the way to the bus stop he went into his blank out mode (not conscious of what he's really thinking or doing) and he had a sixth sense to know everything about people who do wrong to him each day.
 He caught the bus and went to the army surplus store to get some weapons, then went to the drunk guy's house who was in the restaurant being very disrespectful to him (earlier on his job).
 Jake got to the guy's house but he wasn't home, so he waited for him to come home on his back porch.

 It was dusk dark!

Meanwhile the drunk restaurant customer was at a bar on the other side of town.

Chapter 2

The drunk restaurant customer who was at the restaurant where Jake works, was sitting at the bar drinking the drink he ordered for himself.
He wasn't as drunk as he was earlier when he was at the restaurant.
He sobered up a bit but he is at the bar back at it again.
Before long a beautiful young lady by her lonesome came and sat next to him at the bar.
The drunk restaurant customer looked over and responded by saying:

Drunk restaurant customer: Hello sweetheart, how are you?

Lady customer: I'm fine.

Drunk restaurant customer: You are a very beautiful lady!

Lady customer: Thank you.

Drunk restaurant customer: May I ask you your name?

Lady customer: Sure! It's Shelley, what's yours?

Drunk restaurant customer: I'm Joe, do you come here often?

Shelley: Not often but sometimes off and on.

Joe: Can I offer to buy you a drink?

Shelley: Oh! Thank you, but I got it covered. But thanks anyway.

Joe: Aaahhh No! Come on! I insist. It would be my pleasure.

Shelley: OK, if you insist, that will be fine. I would like to have a margarita.

Joe ordered her drink and another round for himself!
The music was playing on the jukebox, a fast song came on that they both liked.

Joe: Do you want to dance?

Shelley: Of course, yes.

They laughed, danced as the night went on!
They were having a good time, laughing, talking, drinking, dancing and just enjoying each other's company.
 The night was over then Shelly and Joe made a bond with one another, Joe invited Shelley over to his house.
 She said OK, where do you stay?
 He said Pacific Palisades.
 They both were not driving that day because they knew they would be out drinking and when all is said and done they would have to call a taxi to get home.
They caught a taxi and went to his house.
They arrived at his house, they paid the driver while still in the car, got out of the car talking out aloud.
 And sleeping on the back porch of Joe's house was Jake waiting on him.
 They went inside the house (Joe and Shelley).

Shelley: You have a nice home.

Joe: Thanks! You can have a seat anywhere you wish.

 Shelley sat down on the sofa.

Joe: Would you like to have a drink?

Shelley: Yes.

Joe: Good.

Joe suggested to Shelley that she can put a CD on in the stereo.

Shelley replied: OK!

At that time Joe went into his kitchen to fix the drinks, and Shelley was sitting in the living room.
 She got up walked to the stereo and found something she liked, put it on and started dancing by herself to the music, passing time until Joe come back with the drinks.

 While Joe was fixing the drinks in his kitchen, the noise (of Joe fixing the drinks and the music playing on the stereo) awakened Jake who was snoozing on Joe's back porch.
 He sat up and started listening and in his shoulder bag was all kinds of weapons.
 Jake got up very quietly, walked to the kitchen window and quietly looked in.
 He saw Joe in the kitchen fixing drinks and at that time he walked to the back door very quietly and carefully picked the back door lock.
 Very quietly and carefully, he got inside the house and was standing in the back of Joe.
Joe sensed something behind him and turned around and Jake grabbed his hair, pulled it up and cut his head off, stuck it in a plastic bag and put it in his shoulder bag and walked out of the back door of the house and was long gone.

The volume of the music was so loud, it drowned out what was going on in the kitchen.
Shelley danced through 2 songs and was getting ready to play another one.
 So, she started to wonder what was taking Joe so long to fix the drinks, she called his name out aloud.
 Joe, Joe, what's the holdup?

She repeated calling his name to no avail.
She went to the kitchen opened the swinging doors and discovered Joe bleeding profusely on the floor dead without his head.
She screamed so loud and started running out of the house.

She was so hysterical she just kept running until she came somewhat to her senses and went and knocked on a neighbor's door, screaming help, help, etc.
The door opened!
A man answered saying what's wrong.
Shelley said my friend was just killed.

Neighbor: Where and who is your friend? Are you OK? Calm down, come in and have a seat.

Shelley: His house is four houses down I think and he is in his kitchen on the floor. His head is cut off and his body is lying on the kitchen floor.

Neighbor: Oh my GOD! Are you sure?

Neighbor: What's your name?

Shelley: My name is Shelley!

Shelley: Yes, I'm sure!

Neighbor: Well, let me call the police.

Shelley: Good! (She is still very scared and hysterical) Thank you.

The police were called!
They arrived at the gentleman's house where Shelley wound up at running to for help.
The police talked with the gentleman and Shelley, got all of

the information they needed to get.

They proceeded to go and locate Joe's house with Shelley's directions, even though she was still shook up.

Together they located where Joe's house was, and they went in and started investigating.

The crime lab and the coroner were called in also.

They talked with Shelley, and they released her but told her not to leave town because they might have some more questions for her.

In the meantime, across town Jake was on his way to find an isolated location where he would keep his bag and remains at, he found one.

That's where he put his stuff and buried the head as a souvenir.

Then on the way home he still was not his real self but he goes to where he lives and uses the bathroom, takes his clothes off and goes to bed, wakes up the next morning not remembering anything that happened the night before.

He's a bachelor, lives by himself, he was getting ready for work and was cleaning his pockets out of the pants he wore yesterday and got his loose change but he remembers everything in being his real self.

He smiled when he saw the bent quarter and he decided just to carry and keep it in his pocket and don't spend it.

For as long as he kept that quarter it never while he had it in his hand or in his pocket or sitting it anywhere else, it never moved around again.

The reason the coin didn't move anymore is because a demonic spirit attacked the coin while in the register at the coffee shop and disfigured it while stored inside the register.

Inside the coin was put a demonic spell on the coin that the first person to hold it will receive the curse from the coin into the person who holds it in their possession for a certain length of time and it was Jake, not the cashier because she just picked it up and handed it to him.

She didn't hold it long enough.

The reason for the coin shaking is that it was releasing the evil spirits into the person, who was holding it for a while which was Jake.
 After it has released the evil spirits it will stay in Jake, until someone can find out the truth about why he's doing what he's doing.
 And if so, he would need an exorcist for being possessed.
 If they don't find out the truth about want's going on with him (doing these type of crimes), someone in the Law Enforcement Agency would have to shoot him with some silver bullets until he is dead, and the demons would leave. Because that is the protocol of a person doing those type of crimes in the eyesight of the Law Enforcement Agencies.

Chapter 3

 Jake got ready for work and was heading out of his apartment, his neighbor was sitting out front on the patio of the apartment building.

Jim (Neighbor): Good morning Jake!

Jake: Good morning Jim! I'm on my way there.

Jim: OK! Have a good day. Check you later.

Jake: OK Thanks! You too.

 He walks to the same bus stop where he catches the bus every time he goes to work.
He boards the bus.

Jake: (speaking to the bus driver) Hello, how are you doing?

Bus driver: OK, how are you?

Jake: I'm good.

 Jake went and had a seat on the bus.
Jake took a seat across from a middle age Caucasian woman.
 Jake got comfortable in his seat and just gave a casual look to her but the woman was very belligerent and responded by saying, what are you looking at nigger?

Jake said: "What! I didn't mean any harm ma'am" and he moved to another seat away from her to keep the peace.

 He went to work and finished the day at work.
 Upon leaving work, Jake went into his blank out mode and the next thing you know he was at the Caucasian woman's house, who he had the run in with earlier on the bus on his

way to work.
 He was waiting for her to get home.
 She lived in a cottage house close to the beach.
 Jake was sitting in her backyard waiting, with his shoulder
bag full of weapons.
Jake had a specially made sword and other different tools to
do his killings and other special made tools for everything
else.

It was dusk dark!

 A light came on in the kitchen.
 Jake got up and quietly walked to the window to confirm who
was inside and it was indeed the Caucasian woman, who he
had the run in with earlier.
 He went in his pocket quietly and got a tool to open her
backdoor quietly.

 (The TV was on and that muffled the sound of the door
opening).
 She was starting to cook something on the stove.
 Jake was behind her and touched her right shoulder.

She was very startled!

 She turned around immediately to her right side, saying
hysterically O00oohhh, with her mouth wide open.
 When she made a complete turn Jake with one of his special
weapons, cut her tongue out of her mouth, pushed her down,
cut off both of her hands, and slit her throat from ear to ear
putting the body parts of hers in special bags he had.
He walked out of her house through the backdoor while she
was on the floor in excruciating pain, rolling around
uncontrollably.

Meanwhile fast forward: The woman was dead for a while
(days), she lived alone.

Her family members were concerned that nobody heard from her in a while.
They checked on her and found her dead mutilated body.
The authorities were called out, but nothing became of the investigation.

Back to Jake and disrespectful woman:

He went home with the body parts he took from the woman, used them as meat for seasoning in a pot of stew.
Ate it all, got full, watched a little TV, cleaned up everything and fell asleep.
He woke up the next morning not remembering a thing.

The next morning was a Saturday, his off days were Saturday and Sunday.

On off days Jake generally stays at home close or around 11:00 am and then goes to the Promenade in Santa Monica to perform (singing and playing his guitar), with his box sitting out in front of him on the ground for donations.

That Saturday after his session was over, a person from an evil empire was listening to Jake's music in the crowd.
He was keeping tabs on Jake to see if the curse from the quarter is working on him.
In the meantime they knew (evil empire) that he acquired the quarter.
Jake got all of his equipment together and money and went home and didn't have a clue what kind of person was part of his audience.

When he got home he put most of his money away in his stash place, took some spending money with him, fixed a sandwich, and ate it, relaxed for a while, left his guitar at home and headed out walking towards the beach.

He walked to the Santa Monica Pier.

It was a nice, warm and sunny day to do it (walk to Pier), a good day to be at the Pier.

When he got there he bought himself an ice cream cone and sat on one of the benches looking out towards the beach and ocean, checking out the crowd on the beach swimming, sunbathing, people sailing in their sailboats and folks riding in their yachts.

He was there for only a short time when three drunk homeless guys were passing by walking in the back of Jake as he was sitting.

One of the three drunk guys recognized Jake from performing on the promenade and he blurted out:

"Hey guitar man what are you doing sitting here?"

Jake: Just got finished performing not too long ago, I'm just out chillin for a while.

Drunk man: Being belligerent he says chillin. It ain't no time for no chillin. Go home and get that guitar and come back and play us something.

Jake: Just trying to relax!

Drunk man: I ain't playing punk, go get that guitar and come back here and play us some music- faggot.

Jake: Hey man, I don't know you. Why are you bothering me? You should learn how to respect people. Jake walked off furious.

Drunk man: That's right punk, you better leave and make sure you come back with that guitar.

Jake left and went to a movie to cool down about what just

happened.

While at the Theatre concession stand, he was standing in front of a pretty girl.

He turned around and said Hello to her.

Lady: Hello!

Jake: How's your day?

Lady: Fine, how's yours?

Jake: Great. By the way what's your name?

Lady: Carolyn, what's yours?

Jake: Jake, pleased to meet you.

Carolyn: Same here.

Jake: Which movie are you going to see?

Carolyn: The Titanic.

Jake: That's what I am here to see too! I was wondering if it would be okay with you for us to watch the movie together.

Carolyn: OK, I don't mind.

Jake: OK, let me be a gentleman and it would be my pleasure to treat you to anything you want at the concession stand.

Carolyn: Ooh! That's very kind of you.

Jake: Well, it would be my pleasure.

Carolyn: OK, that would be fine.

They got their food at the concession stand and went in and found good seats and sat together and watched the movie.
 Every once in a while they would be talking back and forth to one another while the movie was playing.
After the movie they both said great movie and was walking out of the Theatre and Carolyn said:

Carolyn: I have to go use the restroom.

Jake: Me too! Whoever comes out first let's wait for one another at the concession stand. I want to talk to you, so we can talk about whatever comes up.

Carolyn: OK.

Jake came out of the restroom first and Carolyn came out a little while later.
 They met at the concession stand and walked downstairs to the lobby, so they can have a seat in the lounge chairs to chitchat.

Jake: Would you like to have a seat?

Carolyn: Yes. OK, thanks.

 They sat and talked.

Jake: Uuuuhh Carolyn! I'm happy I met you. I can tell you are a nice person and I wouldn't want the time we spent watching the movie together to be in vain and I was wondering if we can do this again.

Carolyn: Sure, I think you are a nice person too.

Jake: Let me give you my cell number. Do you have a cell phone?

Carolyn: Yes, I do

Jake: Is it ok for us to exchange numbers to keep in touch with each other?

Carolyn: Yes, that'll be okay.

They exchanged numbers and said goodnight to each other and that they will keep in touch with one another.

They parted ways!

Jake went home, opened his door and locked his door behind him, turned on the TV, sat down in his chair and went into his blank out mode, left the TV on- (volume not high) opened his door, walked out of his apartment turned and locked the door and walked to where the homeless drunk guy camp was.

The guy was asleep.

Jake had his bag of tools with him (nobody sees where or how he gets his bag of tool weapons) Jake standing over the man, pulled a long rod with sharp rotating blade and pushed it in his neck turned the button on the end of the rod cut the man's adams apple out of his neck.

It was stuck to the rod!

Jake pulled the Adam's apple of the rod, put it in a bag then plunged the rod in the man's head and chest until he was dead.
Jake split from the homeless man's spot, went to his stash spot and put up his tool weapons and headed towards, home. When he got back home he fixed some tea for himself and dropped the Adam's apple in it (for flavor) and drank it. When finished, he disposed of everything and went to bed.

In the meantime, one of the dead homeless guy's homeless friend went to his friend's spot that morning (that's his regular routine) and found his friend dead.

He was all messed up about what he saw.

But he managed to get to a telephone and called the police. They came out and investigated, but couldn't find any clues.

But they (Police Officers), did get help for the dead homeless man's friend because he was all messed up about what happened.

P.S. (The dead homeless man's friend would be juicing (drinking alcohol), so much through the course of a day)!

When the Police Officers started asking him questions about his friend's death, he wasn't of no use.

In reality the man would be so inebriated every day, he wouldn't know his left foot from his right.

Chapter 4

That morning Jake arose as usual.
 He didn't remember a thing about the killing.
 He started going through with his regular routine, making breakfast and watching TV.
 He decided to call Carolyn to touch bases with her.
 She answered, they talked and agreed to meet each other at the Pier at 1:00 pm.
 Jake stayed at home until it was time to meet her (Carolyn). They both arrived at the Pier at the same time, saw one another, they walked towards each other, came together and Jake casually hugged and kissed her on the cheek.

Jake: How are you?

Carolyn: Fine and yourself?

Jake: I'm great. Let's see do you want to take on some rides here (at amusement park) on the Pier?

Carolyn: That sounds like fun, of course.

Jake: But first let's get a couple of ice cream cones.

Carolyn: OK.

 They proceeded to walk over to the ice cream stand and when they got there, Jake asked Carolyn!
 "What flavor do you generally get?", as they were looking over the many flavors they had displayed up on the menu board.

Carolyn: I like them all, but I have a taste for strawberry sherbet.

Jake: I have a thing for butter pecan.

Carolyn: (chuckled) that's good!

Jake: Well, what can I say?

 Carolyn wanted strawberry sherbet and Jake wanted butter pecan.
 Jake ordered their ice cream cones, paid for them and when they received their cones, they went and had a seat at a table in the food court area.
 They were having a pleasant conversation about their past, present lives and future plans.
 Afterwards they went on the rides.
 They rode just about every ride in the park.
 After that they were preparing to leave, they both had to use the restroom.
 Carolyn was out of the restroom first, but there was a man trying to rap on her (being fresh) while she was waiting for Jake.

 She kept telling him she was waiting on her friend to come out of the restroom, but he was trying to force the issue by trying to grab her arm, and at that time Jake walked out of the restroom and saw what was going on.
 Jake immediately ran over there and yelled at the man to stop bothering his friend.
 The guy turned around and said "my bad" and walked off.
 Jake and Carolyn walked to the Promenade to check out some street performers. Before they parted each other's company, saying they enjoyed one another's company, they agreed to stay in touch.

 They went their separate ways.

On his way to his apartment!
 Jake went into his blank out mode, went to his stash spot where he kept his bags of tools and weapons, retrieved the

tools and weapons, he's going to need to do this job that he is getting ready to perform.

He put them in his bag and headed toward the bus stop.

Jake caught a bus towards Malibu, got off on Sunset Blvd. and Ocean Avenue, walked across the street, entered the restaurant and bar establishment, that's where the man is who was stalking Carolyn on the Pier.

Jake knew where he was in the place, he stayed out of view of him.

Jake ordered a cranberry juice and was sipping on it real slow at the bar.

Jake was waiting for his chance to get him and do some harm to him.

The man was sitting at a table eating and drinking, a little while later he got up to go use the restroom.

Jake followed him in the restroom a few minutes behind him. (No one else was in the restroom).

The man was sitting in one of the stalls taking care of his business.

Jake took out one of his tool weapons kicked the bathroom stall door open where the man was sitting.

He was very startled, and then the man hollered "what the fuck" when he opened his mouth, Jake rushed in on him and cut his tongue out, held it in his hand and swung down with his tool and cut his penis off, grabbed it and held it in his hand also, then he repeatedly stabbed the man in his head and chest until he was dead.

Jake put everything up in his bag and walked out of the restaurant.

A little while later an employee at the restaurant had to use the restroom and he discovered the man dead, sitting on the toilet in one of the stalls.

He (employee) reported it to his boss.

The police was called out but nothing ever became of the investigation.

Back to Jake:

Jake went home and made a stew with the body parts that he got from the man who was bothering Carolyn.
He sat down and ate it, watched a little TV and went to bed after cleaning up everything.
As usual the next morning Jake didn't remember a thing about the killing he did the night before.
 All that week Jake went to work until the weekend, without any incidents where he would have to kill someone.

 That Saturday he called his friend Carolyn and invited her to meet him on the Promenade because he was going to perform, playing his guitar and singing.
 He was at his spot performing about 15 minutes on the Promenade.
 He had a few people observing.
 It takes about a half hour to get a full crowd.
 At that time he saw Carolyn walk up.
 After the song he was performing he called her over, to say hello and that he would be here for at least two hours.

Carolyn: OK! I might go look around in a few shops, maybe. If so, I'll be back before you leave.

Jake: OK, let me get back to work, sweetheart!

Carolyn: OK.

Carolyn stayed and listened a while to Jake's performance and then she went browsing around for something to buy.
 Jake performed and took a break and a man named Johnnie started having a conversation with him.

Johnnie: Hello Jake, (Johnnie knew his name because Jake had some business cards sitting out in front of him, Johnnie picked one up) here's my card (card read Johnnie Wilcox with his address and phone number, Corporation Esq.) I was wondering do you make house calls to perform?

Jake: Yes, I do! Depending on the function and location.

Johnnie: It's a birthday party for my daughter, in Pacific Palisades.

Jake: OK, that sounds good.

Johnnie: You have my card and I have yours too. Give me a call and I'll give you all the details.

Jake: OK, that's good. Will do. Pleased to meet you.

Johnnie: Same here. Will talk to you later.

Jake: OK! And have a good day.

Johnnie: OK! Thanks and you too.

Then Johnnie walked off.
Jake started performing again until it was time to leave.
By that time Carolyn had made it back with a few items she bought.
Jake was getting his equipment together and Carolyn walked over and asked if he needed any help.

Carolyn: Do you need any help?

Jake: Yes I do. Thanks.

Carolyn: OK, what do you want me to do?

Jake: Help me put my equipment in your car and then we can go over to this cozy little restaurant I know and get a bite to eat.

Carolyn: OK! Great, I have a little appetite.

Jake: OK! Good, me too. Treat is on me. They have some good food there.

Carolyn: Good, I can't hardly wait.

When they got to her car, Jake complemented Carolyn on how nice her car is.
(She have a Mid-Size Powder Blue Convertible BMW)
Jake and Carolyn working together, to put Jake's equipment in her car.
(Carolyn's car was parked in the parking structure!)
When they were done they started walking towards the restaurant not too far from where he was performing, went in and had a seat.
While waiting for the waiter, they started having a conversation with one another!

Jake: I had a good day.

Carolyn: Good!

Jake: One guy gave me his business card. He wants me to perform at a party. I told him that I like the idea and location of the party and that I would give him a call for all the details.

Carolyn: That sounds great. I think you should follow through with it.

Jake: I think I will. I'll let you know what's going on and if everything is OK, I would like for you to give me a little help and a ride to transport my equipment to the function.

Carolyn: Of course, I would be honored to.

Jake: OK, good.

They sat and ate, enjoying each other's company, talking about different things.
It was a very comfortable setting for the both of them.
After they were through eating, they sat for a while talking, before it was time for them to go.
They proceeded to exit out of the restaurant to Carolyn's car on the way to walking towards her car, Carolyn thanked Jake for the dinner and having a wonderful time.

Jake replied: You're welcome! It was my pleasure and thank you.

Carolyn dropped Jake home and helped him with bringing his equipment to and inside his apartment.
While inside she was standing at the front door, but briefly looked around and said you have a nice place.

Jake: Thank you. I would invite you to stay but we can set a date later for you to come over, when we can spend more time together.

Carolyn: That's fine with me.

Jake embraced her and gave her a kiss on the cheek and said.

Jake: Thanks for everything, and have a safe trip home.

Carolyn: And thank you I had a really good time, I will be safe.

Carolyn departed, Jake closed the door behind her and locked it.
He picked up his equipment a piece at a time, which was sitting by the front door and proceeded to put everything away.
He turned on the TV, sat and relaxed for a while.
Then he retrieved the business card of Johnnie Wilcox out of

his wallet and gave him a call.

(Phone ringing four times)

Johnnie's wife answers: Hello.

Jake: Yes, may I speak to Mr. Johnnie Wilcox?

Johnnie's wife: Hold on one second and let me get him. May I ask who is calling?

Jake: Yes, Jake Wilson. We met on the Promenade and he wanted me to perform for his daughter's upcoming birthday party.

Johnnie's wife: Oh yes! Good, I am her mother.

Jake: Oh! Good, pleased to talk to you.

Johnnie's wife: Same here, hold on a second and let me get him.

Jake: Okay, thanks.

Johnnie: Hello Jake, how are you?

Jake: I'm great, how are you?

Johnnie: Everything's good. So, can you do the party?

Jake: Yes, I think I can. Can you give me the details?

Johnnie: OK, it's for my daughter as you know. Her name is Jesse and she's turning 18. She love's your kind of music, but she don't know who you are and she never heard you play. It will be a treat for her and for her friends. For three hours, take your breaks when you want and I'll pay you $200 an hour flat rate. The day of the party which is a week from now on July 1st which is her birthday and it will fall on a Saturday. Will start at 7:00 pm and go until 10:00 pm. The day of the party call me and I will give you directions on how to get here. Sounds good?

Jake: Yes, everything sounds good. I'll give you a call July 1, in the morning for directions.

Johnnie: OK good. Take care and talk to you then.

Jake: OK, I will you too, bye.

Johnnie: OK, bye.

Jake called Carolyn to tell her about the gig and to ask a few questions.

(Phone ringing)

Carolyn: Hello (in a sensual and sexy tone)

Jake: Hello Carolyn.

Carolyn: Yes, who is it?

Jake: It's Jake! WOW you sound good! I am happy to see you made it home safe.

Carolyn: Oh, Hi Jake. Yes I did make it here safe. Thanks, how are you? What's up?

Jake: I'm good. I was calling to let you know that I took that birthday party gig. It's on July 1st from 7 to 10:00 pm on a Saturday.

Carolyn: That's good.

Jake: I'm going to earn $600 for three hours' work.

Carolyn: WOW, that's great.

Jake: But Carolyn, I might need a ride to get there and back.

Carolyn: OK, that's fine. Just call me and let me know what you want me to do ahead of time, so I can be available.

Jake: Oh, thanks sweetheart. I appreciate it very much. Will do. I will call ahead of time and let you know. And thanks again.

Carolyn: You're welcome, no worries.

Jake: OK, good. Will talk to you soon. Be safe.

Carolyn: OK you too, bye.

Jake: OK, bye.

 Time went on for Jake without any major incidents to where he would have to kill someone.
 Before he knew it, it was that Friday before the birthday party. He was at home that night (Friday) and he called Carolyn to touch bases.

(Phone ringing)

Carolyn: Hello.

Jake: Hello Carolyn.

She recognizes his voice now.

Carolyn: Hello Jake, how are you?

Jake: I'm good. I just called to find out if you can drop me off and pick me up at the Birthday party tomorrow.

Carolyn: Yes, I'll be free. What time do you want me to be there?

Jake: Let me get back with you tomorrow morning, after I call Mr. Wilcox to get directions and I'll give you a call.

Carolyn: OK.

Jake: Will talk to you soon. Be safe.

Carolyn: OK you too, bye.

Jake: OK, bye.

After talking to Carolyn, Jake retired for the night.
 The next morning he woke up around 8:00 am, washed up, had breakfast while watching TV.
 When he finished eating, he rested for a while, kicking back watching TV and decided to call Mr. Wilcox.
They talked and Mr. Wilcox gave him the directions.
 They were fairly easy and simple directions from Jake's house to Mr. Wilcox's house.
Everything was set for the party.
 All Jake had to do is to call Carolyn and tell her what time to pick him up and he did.
 It was for 5:30 pm on July 1.
Jake just kicked it at home that day (July 1st) until it was time to leave.
 At 5:00 pm his phone rang and it was Carolyn.

Jake: Hello.

Carolyn: Hi Jake, its Carolyn. What's your address so I can be on my way over?

Carolyn: I know, I've been there before but I want to be sure.

Jake: Hi Carolyn, its 1220 9th Street, #Z in Santa Monica.

Carolyn: OK, good. I know the area and will be there shortly.

Jake: Great, will see you soon. Be safe, bye.

Carolyn: OK, bye.

Carolyn was there in 15 minutes.
 It was 5:15 pm.
 She called Jake from her cell phone outside his apartment to let him know that she was out front.
 He said OK, will be right out.
 He walked out front, there she was sitting in her Blue Convertible BMW.
 He walked up to the car and said:

Jake: Hello Carolyn, that was fast. I just can't stop telling you how much I like your car.

Carolyn: Hi Ok, Thank you! Yes, I like it too (her car), I don't live too far from here. I'm on Wilshire and Yale.

Jake: You're right, that's right up the street. Before we leave let's go inside for a moment, so you can see my shack.

Carolyn: OK.

She got out of her car, locked it, walked towards him, they embraced and a respectful hug and he gave her a kiss on the cheek.
 She said thank you.

Jake: Come on, let me show you my ponderosa.

Carolyn: Slight chuckle, OK.

So they walked to his apartment.

Jake: Come on in.

Carolyn: WOW! Your shack is nice. Nice color carpet, nice furniture and I like your bike.

Jake: That's the kitchen (pointing to his right) and that's the restroom (pointing to his left).

Carolyn: Nice, nice. I like your place.

Jake: Thank you. Were early but, I think it's about time for us to be leaving for the party.

Carolyn: OK, whenever you're ready.

So Jake and Carolyn worked together to put his equipment in her car from his place.

Jake: Can you make out these directions to the house where the party is?

Jake handed the directions to Carolyn. She looked them over and said:

Carolyn: Yes, good. I know this area. No worries.

Jake: OK, good. Let's rock and roll.

Carolyn: OK.

They got in her car and headed towards Pacific Palisades

where the Party is.
 They arrived there early.
 Jake got his instruments and equipment out of the car and sat them on the ground.
 She stood out of the car in front of the house.
 They hugged and said their goodbyes.

Carolyn: I'll be back here for 10:00 pm.

Jake: Great, if you run into any problems, give me a call.

Carolyn: OK, I hope not.

Jake: Me too, but be safe.

Carolyn: I will! You too and you have a lot of fun.

Jake: Will do. See you later.

Carolyn: OK, bye

 Carolyn got into her car and took off and Jake grabbed his gear and walked to the front door and rang the bell.

 Mrs. Wilcox answered the door.

Mrs. Wilcox: Hello, you must be Jake. Come on in you are early.

Jake: OK, thank you, you must be Mrs. Wilcox.

Mrs. Wilcox: Yes I am.

Jake: Yes I am early I just wanted to get a feel of the area but you don't have to pay me for the time it's on me. Where do you want me to set up my equipment?

Mrs. Wilcox: OK! I understand you would like to get the feel of the place, come on and let me show you where to set up. Did you have any trouble finding our place?

Jake: No, I didn't. I have a friend that is familiar with the area and it wasn't a problem at all.

Mrs. Wilcox: OK, good! Mrs. Wilcox and Jake proceeded to walk towards the patio.

Mrs. Wilcox: You can set your stuff under the awnings on the patio. This is it. Just find you a good spot to set up because the party is going to be out here in the backyard.

Jake: Cool, this looks great. I'll start setting up now.

Mrs. Wilcox: OK, good. Do you want anything to drink or snack on?

Jake: Yes, whatever you have I'll appreciate it.

Mrs. Wilcox: OK, I'll be right back with something.

Jake: OK, thanks.

Jake started to set up his equipment and Mrs. Wilcox came back with drink and snacks.

Mrs. Wilcox: Here's to you. I hope you like lemonade and Chex mix.

Jake: I do! Thank you very much.

Mrs. Wilcox: You're welcome. Uuhh Johnnie is at the office. He should be home in a few minutes. When he gets here I'll let him know you're out here on the patio. My daughter is at the mall with her friends. She'll be home a little later. Is everything okay, Jake?

Jake: Yes, everything's OK. I'll just get a little practice in for now.

Mrs. Wilcox: OK, if you need me I'll be inside.

Jake: OK, Thanks.

Jake went over a few songs for about 15 minutes and in came Mr. Wilcox.

. Mr. Wilcox: Hey guy, how is everything?

Jake: It's all good. Just got finished going over a few songs.

Mr. Wilcox: Yes, I heard a little of it. It sounds good. Are you ready to rock the house (He smiles)?

Jake: Yes, I'm ready to rock the house (He smiles).

At that time guests started to arrive, and started mingling around.

Mr. Wilcox: I'll talk to you later Jake. Guests are arriving. Whenever you are ready you can start.

Jake: OK, I'll be ready in about 10 minutes.

At the time a bunch of young boys and girls were mingling in a crowd and one girl stepped away from the crowd towards Jake and introduced herself.

Girl: Hello, my name is Jesse. This is my Birthday Party.

Jake: OK, my name is Jake. I'm pleased to meet you.

 My first song will be the Happy Birthday song to you and afterwards we are going to rock the house.
Jesse is so Happy and delighted with Jake, his mannerisms, charm and good looks.
She was one very happy young lady on her Birthday.

Jesse: Oh, great! When will you start?

Jake: In about five minutes.

Jesse: OK, good. She ran off into the crowd bouncing up and down, extremely delighted talking to friends and she can't hardly wait for the show to start.

Jake sang the Happy Birthday song and the crowd joined in, wishing Jesse a Happy Birthday.
 She was so happy!
She kept saying, Thank you to Jake and guests with friendly hugs.
Afterwards Jake started jammin.
 Everybody was having a wonderful time, dancing, singing along, laughing, etc.
But at Jake's first break, Jesse came over to talk to Jake.

Jesse: You're good. I love your music.

Jake: Thank you. I appreciate it.

Jesse: How did my parents find you?

Jake: I generally play on the Third Street Promenade in Santa Monica. One day your father was on the Promenade and he introduced himself and gave me his card. He asked me to give him a call because he wanted to hire me to perform at a birthday party. Well, here I am.

Jesse: (She's chuckling). I'm glad because I really like your music. Are you still performing on the Promenade?

Jake: Yes, every Saturday and Sunday from Noon to 3:00 pm if the weather permits.

Jesse: Oh, OK I'd like to come there to see you perform.

Jake: OK, I'll tell you what. I'll give you my cell phone number. Do you have a cell phone?

Jesse: Yes, I do.

Jake: Well before I leave today, we will swap numbers so we can be in touch with one another.

Jesse: Cool that would be perfect.

Jake: Well, let me get back to playing.

Jesse: OK, I will get your number at your next brake.

Jake: Cool, enjoy the music.

Jesse: I will. Thanks.

 She went back into the crowd!
 Jake started performing again and at the end of the gig (party), they swapped numbers and Jake said:

Jake: We'll keep in touch and I'll let you know my schedule to keep you up to date.

Jesse: OK, cool. I really enjoying my Birthday, Thanks in part to you with your performance and for sure I will keep in touch.

Jake: OK, That's good. I'll do the same thing.

Jesse walked off while Jake was getting his gear together, before he gave Carolyn a call to come pick him up.

Then Mr. Wilcox walked up to him with his wife Mrs. Wilcox.

Mr. Wilcox: Thanks very much my man. Did everything go smooth?

Jake: Yes, it did. We all had a ball. By the way I met your daughter and she would like to come see me on the Promenade when I'm performing. We exchanged numbers, is that OK?

Mr. Wilcox: Sure, no worries. I'm happy you guys made friends. Since everything was so great, I am going to give you an extra $100.

Jake: OOoooh! Thank you very much sir. I really appreciate it.

Mr. Wilcox: You're welcome. We appreciate you for giving my daughter a Birthday that she will remember for the rest of her life.

Mrs. Wilcox: Yes and I second that emotion.

Jake: You're welcome. I just try to do my best folks, and Thanks again.

Mr. Wilcox handed Jake his money, $700.00.

Jake replied: Thanks very much, let me finish getting my equipment together and call my friend to come and pick me up.

Mr. Wilcox: OK, don't forget to stay in touch.

Mrs. Wilcox: Yes, please do.

Jake: For sure will do.

Mr. and Mrs. Wilcox walked off back into the house.

Jake made his call to Carolyn.
He said his goodnights to everybody and sat out on the front porch until Carolyn showed up, which was fairly quick.
She pulled up, Jake walked to the car.
Carolyn got out of the car, stood on the sidewalk.
When they met they embrace one another, saying hello to each other and a warm felt hug.
Jake gave her a kiss on the cheek.
After the kiss, Jake started putting his equipment in Carolyn's car with the help of Carolyn and they drove off.
They are having a conversation as they are riding!

Carolyn: How was everything?

Jake: Everything was great. I got a $100 bonus for giving a good show.

Carolyn: Wow! Real good. I gather everyone had a great time?

Jake: Yes, I did also.

Carolyn: Good, you look a little tired.

Jake: Yes, I am tired. Going in, eat a snack and get ready for bed. I'm tired.

Carolyn: OK, we should be there shortly. They got to the house. Carolyn stayed in the car, Jake gave her a kiss on the cheek, got out, retrieved his equipment out of the car, said goodbye to Carolyn and said to her to be safe and to call him when she got home.

She replied, will do.
 Carolyn calling Jake, when she got home.

(Phone ringing)

Jake: Hello

Carolyn: Hello Jake, this is Carolyn.

Jake: I know, I recognize your voice now.

Carolyn: OK, good. I made it home safe.

Jake: OK great. Have a good night. Will talk to you later and be safe.

Carolyn: OK, you too. Bye.

Jake: Bye

Chapter 5

Time passed on as days went by, Jake was still working at the restaurant and performing on Saturdays and Sundays and was still an acquaintance with Carolyn.

 And not too long after the party!

 Jesse was visiting him off and on at the Promenade to see him perform on Sundays.
But one weekend on a Saturday when Jake was getting ready to set up his equipment on the Promenade, Carolyn as usual was there, that was her regular schedule to be there when he first set up.
She would listen for a little while and on the first break, tells

Jake she's going shopping and she'll be back.
Sometimes she comes back and sometimes she doesn't.
And Jesse usually comes to see him perform on Sundays.
Sometimes she stays until the end of the performance,
sometimes she doesn't.
But this particular Saturday they both showed up at the same
time.
Jake was getting ready to perform he was setting up his
equipment.
Almost simultaneously Carolyn and Jesse walked up, one
behind the other to say hello to Jake.
Jake had his head down!

Carolyn: Hello Jake.

Jake looked up!

Jesse: Hello Jake.

Now he's looking at both Carolyn and Jesse.
He was shocked! But he keep his cool.

Jake: Hello ladies. Carolyn I'd like for you to meet Jesse.
She's the young lady I performed for at her birthday party.
Jesse, I'd like for you to meet Carolyn. She's a very close and
good friend of mine.

Carolyn: Pleased to meet you, Jesse.

Jesse: Pleased to meet you, Carolyn.

Carolyn: Uh Jake, I'll be back soon. Going to see if I can catch
a good sale. Uh nice meeting you, Jesse.

Jesse: Same here, hope you can find a good deal.

Carolyn: Thanks. Catch you guys later.

Jake: OK, be safe.

Jesse: OK, see you later (talking to Carolyn).

Jesse: Is that your girlfriend, Jake?

Jake: No, just a close friend, why do you ask?

Jesse: Just curious. I'm not going to stay today. Just came to say hello and to wish you well and for you to rock the house.

Jake: OK, Thanks and I will call you later and be safe.

Jesse: OK, I will.

Jesse walked off down the Promenade and Jake got everything set up and started jamming.
About a half an hour before Jake was finished jamming, Carolyn showed up with a bunch of bags from shopping.
When he stopped playing the song he was performing, Carolyn told him she was going to put all of her shopping bags in her car and she'll be right back.
Jake said OK.
It was time for Jake to pack up and leave, he was getting his equipment together and
Carolyn walked up.

Carolyn: Are you just about ready to leave?

Jake: In a few minutes.

Carolyn took a seat on the bench right next to where Jake was performing and just relaxed and waited until he was finished breaking down his equipment.
In the meantime in the middle of him getting his equipment together, he was casually talking to people who was listening

to his music about different things.
 He got all of his equipment together and he was ready to leave.

Jake: All set, let's get out of here.

Carolyn: OK ready, alright (stretching her arms) let's go.
Carolyn helped Jake to carry his equipment to her car, so she can drop him off at his place.

 They went and put the equipment in Carolyn's car and she drove him home.
They arrived at Jake's house, Carolyn helped him to put his equipment on his front porch.

Carolyn: I'm not going to stay, I'm a little tired.

 They embraced and hugged one another and Jake gave her a kiss on the cheek.

Jake: OK, call me when you get home, to let me know that you made it home safe.

Carolyn: OK, will do.

 Carolyn went home and when she got in she called Jake and told him she made it home okay.
 But little did she know at no surprise, Jesse was waiting for her in her closet.
 Carolyn was getting comfortable in her apartment, getting dinner prepared, turned on the TV and went to her bedroom to hang up the clothes that she bought.
 She opened the closet door and Jesse attacked her, just like Jake with special tools of weapons, and plucked Carolyn's eyes out, stuffed them in a bag, pulled out another weapon and cut off her cheeks on her face and cut off her ears, cut out her tongue and cut her arms off.

She stuffed them all in a bag and walked out, leaving Carolyn flopping around on the floor like a fish out of water and left her for dead.

Jesse made it to her parent's house.

With all the human parts she collected she fixed a stew and had dinner (her parents were not home).

And just like Jake, she cleaned up after herself, rested for a while.

(Both Jesse and Jake had specially made tools).

She went to bed just like Jake, didn't remember a thing about the murder of Carolyn she just committed.

The next morning Jesse awakened to the smell of bacon cooking in the kitchen which her mother was making.

Jesse arose, got cleaned up and went downstairs to the kitchen where her mother was cooking.

Jesse: Good morning Mother!

Mrs. Wilcox (Mother): Good morning sweetheart, how was your day yesterday?

Jesse: It was great Mother. I went to the Santa Monica Promenade and I saw and talked to Jake while he was setting up his equipment.

I didn't stay to see him perform, I decided to go shopping.

Mrs. Wilcox: Did you get to talk to him?

Jesse: Yes, I did.

Mother: Do you like Jake?

Jesse: He's alright.

Mother: That means you like him.

Jesse: Noooo Mother! Stop putting words in my mouth.

Mother: I'll tell you what, Ooh! Do you want some breakfast?

Jesse: Yes, I'll have some.

Mother: Uh, the next time you see Jake, invite him to dinner and tell him it's our invitation to him to get to see and talk to him again.

Jesse: OK, good. I sure will. I'll be going back to the Promenade next Saturday about Noon, if weather permits. He would be already performing.

Mother: OK good, them him to call me or your Dad. I'll let Dad know what's up and we'll set up a time for him to come over.

Jesse: OK, will do. Thanks Mom.

Mother: You're welcome honey. No worries.

Mom fixed breakfast.

Dad came down, saying good morning and they talked as usual about family stuff as they were sitting at the breakfast table having breakfast.
After breakfast, they got themselves together to go to church at the Second Presbyterian Church in Pacific Palisades.
They have been members for years!
They attended church, came home, spent the rest of the day at home.

That Monday!
Mr. Wilcox went to work at his office.
Mrs. Wilcox stayed home.
Jesse is a student at Pepperdine University in Malibu (Biology major).

They all were doing their thing that week.

That Saturday, they were all sitting at the breakfast table.

Jesse: Mom, I am going to Santa Monica today.

Mrs. Wilcox: OK, don't forget to tell Jake to call us. If he doesn't have our number, give it to him.

Jesse: OK, will do.

Mr. Wilcox: Tell him I said hello and be safe out there.

Jesse: OK Dad, I will.

Jesse arrived in Santa Monica, parked her car (A Pink Convertible Mercedes) in the parking structure and walked to the Promenade.
When she got to where Jake is generally playing, he was there as usual (the weather was good).
She walked up on the middle of one of his performances, but he did acknowledge that she was there by nodding his head to her.
When the song was over she walked over to him, said Hello and that she was going to stay around until it is time for him to go.
She said it was important and had something to tell him.

Jake: OK, sounds good.

When Jake's session was over Jesse told him.

Jesse: My parents want you over for dinner this afternoon and they want you to call them.

Jake: OK, let me get everything situated here and there is something I want to ask you.

Jesse: OK.

 Jake got all of his equipment together him and Jesse walked a little ways to the beach and had a seat on a bench by the bluffs.   ,
 (His equipment was easy to carry).
 He asked her would she like to go to a movie in a few minutes on the Promenade.

Jesse: Yes, I would love too.

Jake: OK, good. Let me call your parents and let them know we are going to take on a movie and then we will go to your house for dinner.

Jesse: OK. Do you have their number?

Jake: Yes, I do.

Jake, called Jesse's parents and told them the plan about them going to a movie afterwards and they will head toward their house for dinner.

Jake: Jesse, can I put my equipment in your car before we go to the movie?

Jesse: Of course, no worries.

 They left the park and started walking towards her car, to put up his equipment.
When they got close to her car, she pointed at it (her car) and said:

Jesse: That's me!

Jake looked at her car and replied:

Jake: WOW! That's a bad ride!

Jesse: (chuckled) Thank you.

Jake: You're welcome.

They proceeded to put his equipment in her car.
When they were done, they started walking towards the
Theatre,
On the way to the Theatre, Jake said to Jesse:

Jake: There is a good movie playing starring George Clooney
and Julie Roberts. I heard it is supposed to be good. Let's
check that one out.

Jesse: OK, sounds good.

They went to see the movie and when they got out of the
Theatre, they were very pleased.

Jake: That was a good movie.

Jesse: Yes, it was.

They started walking towards Jesse's car.
On their way to Jesse's car, a drunk guy who knew Jake from
performing on the Promenade starting acting belligerent and
disrespectful.

Drunk guy: Hey guitar man, nice lady you're with. Hey man
help me out with a little change.

Jake: Thanks man, this is my friend. Right now I can't help
you.

At the same time, Jesse said Thank you to the drunk man for

the compliment.

Drunk man: Guitar man, you ain't about shit. You ain't shit. I know you have some money. You just trying to impress that bitch you're with.

Jake: What? Hey man, watch your mouth.

At the same time, Jesse was in awe and got very scared.

Jake: Come on Jesse, let's get out of here.

 They started to trot off from him.

Drunk man: That's right. Run your punk ass off you and that bitch.

 Jake and Jesse went to the parking structure where her car was, got in and drove off, headed for her house.

 (Jesse is driving)!

On their way driving to her house, Jake said:
Jake: Can you believe that? What just happened?

Jesse: No I can't. Did you know that guy?

Jake: Not really. I've seen him around but never really kicked it with him.

Jesse: What do you mean by never kicked it with him?

Jake: (a hardy laugh) Ha Ha Ha Ha Ha Ha Ha. That's funny. No kicking it means hanging out with them, talking maybe drinking beer, just hanging out together and talking about different things.

Jesse: Oh, OK. I understand.

Jake: You don't know too many slang words, do you?

Jesse: No! (Smiling slightly)

Jake: No worries. When you can't recognize or know the meaning of one, I'll let you know.

Jesse: OK Thanks! That's good.

They arrived at Jesse's parents' house. Jesse opened the front door, hollering Mom- Dad.

Mom: We're in the kitchen.

Jesse and Jake walked to the kitchen, pushed the door open simultaneously.

Mom and Dad together saying Hello guys, how was the movie?

Jesse: It was great. I'm not going to tell you anything about it because I don't want to spoil it for you guys. I want you guys to go see it.

Dad: OK, honey (to his wife). Would you like to go see it?

Mom: Sure, Jesse. What's the name of it?

Jesse told them the name of the movie and who was starring in it.

Jake told them what Theatre it was playing at, and to make sure that they got some popcorn and soda pop.
They sat down and had dinner, having casual conversations about different subjects.

When the night was over, it was time for Jake to go home. They said their goodbyes to each other.

Jesse: Are you ready for me to bring you home?

Jake: Yes, whenever you are.

Jesse: OK, I'm ready, let's go.

Jesse talking to her parents. Be right back guys.

Jake: Goodnight and Thanks very much for everything and the dinner was very delicious, GOD Bless the cook (everyone laughed).

Mom: Oh, Thanks Jake, it was my pleasure.

Dad: You guys be safe out there traveling.

Jesse and Jake together they said, OK we will.
Jesse dropped Jake off at his apartment.
When they pulled up in front of the apartment, Jake said:

Jake: Well, this is my Ponderosa.

Jesse: (pleasant smile). Yes, nice area and nice place.

They got out of the car.

Jake: I would invite you in but it's been a long day and I'm tired. But next time for sure.

Jesse: OK, that would be fine.

Jake walked over to Jesse and gave her a warm, pleasant hug and kiss, retrieved his equipment and said:

Jake: Goodnight Jesse, drive safe. I had a nice time and call me when you get home.

Jesse: Goodnight Jake. I had a nice time too. I will be safe and I will call you when I get there.

Chapter 6

She (Jesse)! Left and she drove to where the homeless man camp is who gave them grief earlier that day.

She parked her car, got out walked cautiously to the homeless man camp to find out that he wasn't there.

So she found a cubby hole to wait for him, with her bag with her special tool weapons, until he got back to go to sleep.

In the meantime Jake was on his way to the same homeless man's spot where he camps.

Little did he know that Jesse was there already in a cubby hole with the same intentions as Jake, to torture, mane and kill the guy and take souvenirs off of his body to take home with them, to either bury or eat them.

Jake checked the area, noticed he wasn't in his spot, he found him a cubby hole not too far away from Jesse to wait until the homeless man came back to go to sleep.

All the while, Jesse or Jake did not know that either one of each other was there waiting for the homeless man to come back to his spot.

A short while passed. It was late at night.

The homeless man was walking and stumbling down the street towards his camp drunk attempting to try to sing a song.

He wasn't feeling no pain.

There wasn't nobody else around.

Jesse and Jake both in their cubby holes, can hear him coming to his spot.

They both waited until he got closer (they both were impatient)!

Suddenly! Jesse jumped out from her cubby hole with her specially made tools of weapons and cut the drunk man's head off, in the middle of the man body falling down and head lying on the ground Jesse stooped over to pick up his head to put it in her bag.

Then Jake came out of his cubby hole, saw what was happening.

Jesse turned to him (Jake) and was astonished, saying ooh ooh.

Jake said: Oh my goodness!

They looked at one another and noticed that each one had similar type tools of weapons and wondering why each other met there with the same purpose in mind.

Nevertheless nothing was said to each other.

Jesse was still holding the homeless man head in her hand, she proceeded to put it in her bag.

Jake cut off his hands and feet and put them in his bag and Jesse cut out his heart and put it in her bag also.

They did what they wanted to do and trotted on the way out of there.

Jesse says! Come on let's go to the car.

They got to the car which wasn't too far away, put their bags in the trunk, and got in the car and drove off.

(Jesse is driving)!
(Jake caught the bus to the homeless man camp)

Jake: Let's go to my house.

Jesse: OK good.

They went to his house.

Jake: Let's bring all the bags inside.

Jesse: OK.

When they got inside, for some strange reason they didn't talk.
They just went to the job at hand, cleaning the body parts to

prepare them for cooking and that would be the meal for the night.
(By the way Jesse kept the head of the homeless man to dispose of it later whichever way she see fit)
While the meal was cooking which Jesse stepped up to fix, they sat around for a while listening to gothic (Macabre) music, and started looking at each other with lust in their hearts.
 They embraced each other, started kissing and began to take off their clothes, laid down on the floor and started to have sex, until the food was ready.
They ate, got full afterwards, cleaned up, took a shower together and had more sex. They fell asleep and woke up the next morning.
 Jesse woke up first and looked over at Jake who was still asleep, she shook him.

Jesse: Jake! Wake up.

Jake: Yea, what's going on?

Jesse: Good morning.

Jake: Good morning.

Jesse: Do you remember what we did last night?

Jake: Don't talk so loud. Yes I do.

The demons that is possessing them is letting them see what they are doing, since they have become together as friends.
 Before, Jesse was doing her evil stuff at an early age, passed on from her parents.
 On the other hand Jake was all new to it.
Jesse's father knew that he (Jake) had possession of the cursed coin and the demonic powers was passed on into him.

Because, Jesse's parents was looking for a husband for Jesse to get married and have children and to keep the evil demonic bloodline going.

Jesse: I don't know what to say.

Jake: I don't neither, but let's keep this to ourselves until we can find out more about what's going on with us.

Jesse: OK, sounds good to me. I'm going home. It's always good to be with you.

Jake: Same here. Call me when you get there and be safe.

Jesse: OK, will do.

On her (Jesse) way home, she buried the head of the homeless man in a field close to where she keeps her stash of tool weapons.
Jesse made it home and called Jake, letting him know she got home safely and invited him over to her house next week for dinner.
He agreed with the invitation and she will call to make plans, when for him to come over.
Jake went on with regular activities.
He was feeling very awkward at work, home and out and around about town, but he wouldn't make it obvious about what he and Jesse did a few days ago.
The next weekend rolled around (which was a Saturday), and Jake called Jesse for a date to go see a movie after he performed and then they would go to her house for dinner.

Jesse: OK, that sounds great. I'm more than sure that would be fine with my parents.
I'll meet you there on the Promenade.

Jake: OK, good. See you then.

Jesse: OK, bye.

Jesse let her parents know that her and Jake have a movie date and will come to the house for dinner afterwards.
 They agreed (the parents) and will have everything ready for them (the dinner) when they arrive.
 Their movie was over, they both enjoyed it.
 When they got to the house (Jesse's parents' home) they expressed it was a good movie, suggested that they should go see it.
 They sat around and talked for a while and before they knew it, it was time for Jesse to drive Jake home.
 But not a word was said from Jesse or Jake about what they did the other week.
As time went on Jake and Jesse were getting closer to each other.
 Every now and then Jake would wonder what happened to Carolyn.
 He was calling her for a while, until one day he called and her phone was disconnected.
Every once in a while he would kind of be missing her, wondering where is she and why she hasn't been coming around and hoping that she's alright.
As time went on with Jake and Jesse's relationship, one day Jesse asked Jake what ever happened to Carolyn.

 He replied:

Jake: I don't know. I tried to call her a few times and at one point her phone was disconnected.

Jesse: Oh, I hope she is alright. She seems to be a nice person.

Jake: Yea, she was alright.

(Jesse knew all the time that she killed Carolyn, she was just playing it off like she is so concern about what happen to her)! Jake didn't have a clue that Jesse killed her.
And so on, Carolyn was never discussed between them again.

As a matter of fact about two weeks after Jesse killed Carolyn, the neighbors of Carolyn were smelling a horrible odor coming from her apartment.
They called the police, explaining the situation to them about the horrible odor coming from her place.
They responded saying okay, we will send a patrol car out to investigate, the neighbor who called replied okay, Thanks.
They arrived and forced their way into her apartment. They found her on the floor lying dead with her body badly mutilated.
They investigated the crime but nothing never became of it.

As time went by, they (Jake and Jesse) kept getting closer doing a lot of different things together, spending a lot of time with each other.
Lo and behold Jesse got pregnant and Jake stepped up to the plate to be a man and accept his responsibilities of getting married and for them both to live and grow together, raising their child.
He (Jake) asked permission for Jesse's hand in marriage from her parents.
They agreed!
That's what the parents wanted all along.

Jake and Jesse's father had a talk about his (Jakes) job, at the restaurant and they both decided that Jake would be better off working for Jesse's father at his place of business in the mailroom. He would make three times the money of what he was making at the restaurant where he was currently working.
(Jake accepted the job at Jesse's father place of business and Jesse parents helped them purchase a home on the other

side of town)

As time went by Jesse is about six months pregnant and in different situations off and on that they (Jake and Jesse) would get into not of their doings, but they would finish it in their usual manner, killing people and retrieving different body parts, to bring home and make a pot of stew to eat.
 When finish, have a little sex- rest awhile and then, go to sleep.
When they (Jake and Jesse) would have time they would go over to Jesse's parents' house to socialize and eat and just to spend quality time with family.
 All the killing Jake and Jesse was doing they were controlling it well.
 But as time went by it was starting to show to Jesse's parents that it was bothering them a little.
 They would be sitting around in the living room, watching TV. The parents excused themselves one day and went into the other room to talk, they decided to tell them everything why they was doing, what they were doing.
The parents came back in the room and said, hey guys there is something we have to tell you.
They had a seat (The Parents) and Mr. Wilcox said:

Mr. Wilcox: Guys the reason you guys have been behaving the way you have...

Jake and Jesse: They interrupted and responded at the same time. What do you mean?

Mr. Wilcox: Let me finish. I know everything you guys have been doing.

Jesse: Serious?

Jake: For real?

Mrs. Wilcox: Johnnie and I know everything you guys have been doing.

Jesse: What's really going on MOM?

Jake: Yea, what's really happening?

Mr. Wilcox: Guys this is what's going on. Our family is with the secret society of the order of the devil (Satan).

Jesse and Jake both jumped up from their seats, looking at the parents, looking around the room, hollering out expletives words walking back and forth for a while until they both (Jesse and Jake), calmed down and sat attentively and directed their undivided attention towards the parents.

 Mr. Wilcox went on to explain to Jesse and Jake more about their lifestyle.

Mr. Wilcox: OK Jesse! Honey the power you have, you've been having that from birth.

Stay calm guys and let me finish telling you guys about the society.

Mr. Wilcox: Jake, the bent coin you got from the cashier when you picked it up, it transferred the powers into you, because what was happening we needed a husband for my daughter to marry and have a child to take over the reigns of the society when of age. Jake we set the whole thing up at the store so you can get the coin.

Jake: What! What's with that Mr. Wilcox?

Jake's standing up in disgust, anger and disappointment.
 He was furious!
Jake stormed out of the house and Jesse right behind him.

She's feeling the same way he was.
They jumped into her car and started driving themselves home.

Back at the house Mr. Wilcox expressed his opinion about them running out of the house to Mrs. Wilcox.

Mr. Wilcox: That's very understandable the way they are acting.

Mrs. Wilcox: I agree.

Mr. Wilcox: They will come around.

Mrs. Wilcox: Yes, I think so too.

On the way driving to their house:
Jake was driving, they (Jake and Jesse) calmed down and came somewhat close to their senses.

Jake: What's wrong with your parents?

Jesse: I don't know. Whatever it is! I don't like it.

They are still driving!

Jake: What are we going to do about this?

Jesse: I don't know. Do you have any ideas?

Jake: Yes, I do.

Jesse: You do! What is it?

Jake: We're almost home. I'll tell you when we get inside the house.

They (Jake and Jesse) arrived to their home- went in and got comfortable.

Jesse went into the bathroom and Jake was sitting on the sofa in deep thought.

When Jesse came out of the bathroom she walked in the living room, she noticed Jake was in a deep thought.

Jesse: What's on your mind honey?

Jake: I'm thinking that we should see a Priest and get an exorcism performed on us to get rid of all these demons in us and it's probably in our baby too.

Jesse: OK, Jake if that's what you want to do I agree, I think it is a very good idea.

Jake: Let's get this done and start a new life for ourselves.

Jesse: I most definitely agree. OK!

Jake searched around for a Priest who can perform the exorcism.

After a couple of weeks later, he located one who has permission from the Vatican to perform the task.

The priest name is Father Milan.

(They are talking on the phone)

He agreed (The Priest) to perform the exorcism for them in their house.

After Jake explained to him the circumstances surrounded the reason for locating him (Father).

Jake: Father, what schedule are you going to set up for us, to get together to plan out the circumstances.

Father: Right now, I'll have to check my schedule and call and let you know. No worries it will just be a day or two.

The both agreed and said there goodbyes on the telephone. One day passed and Father called Jake and Jesse.

(Phone ringing)

They are both home, because it was a weekend. He didn't have to work.

Jesse: Hello.

Father: Hello, yes is Mr. Jake Wilson home?

Jesse: Yes he is. Who's calling?

Father: This is Father Milan.

Jesse: Oh, Hi Father. How are you?

Father: I'm great and yourself?

Jesse: We're fine, I'm Jake's wife, are you calling to set up the appointment?

Father: Yes, please to talk to you, let me speak with your husband please.

Jesse: OK, let me get him, we'll see and talk to you soon, Sir.

Father: OK.

In the background Jesse hollering Jake's name out loud.

Jake: Yea, Jesse?

Jesse: Telephone! It's Father Milan.

Jake walked over to where Jesse was, she handed him the

phone.

It must be the Priest who I talked to who will perform the exorcism.

Jake: Hello Father Milan. How is everything?

Father: Everything is great. Are you guys okay?

Jake: Yes, we are Sir!

Father: OK, good. Here's what's going on. I can be over at your house Tuesday, June 12th at 10:00 am to talk with you, if that's okay for you all?

Jake: Yes Sir, that's a good time.

Father: OK, good. I'll give you a call that morning, to let you know that I'm on my way, and to get your address, so I can get directions on how to get there.

Jake: OK Father, we'll be waiting for your call.

Father: OK good. Talk to you later. Bye.

Jake: OK, bye.

Fast-forward: The next Tuesday morning about 8:15 am. Phone ringing.

Jake: Hello.

Father: Hello Jake. (Jake recognizes the Father's voice.)

Jake: Yes, Hello Father Milan, How are you?

Father: OK, I'm great. Just calling to see if all is okay for today. I will be there at 10:00 am, plus I need for you to give me your address.

Jake said everything is ok and gave him their address, the Father thanked him and said, I'll be there at 10:00 am.

Jake: OK, we will be here. See you then Father.

Father: OK, bye.

Jake: OK, bye.

Father Milan arrived at Jake and Jesse's house at 10:00 am as planned, and rang the bell.
 Jesse answered the door.

Jesse: Hello Father Milan, come on in.

She knew it was him because he had his Priest attire on.

Father: Hi, okay.

They walked to the living room (Jesse and Father Milan).
Jake was sitting on the sofa.
Jake stood up and walked towards Father Milan and they shook hands.

Jake: Hello Father Milan, have a seat.

Father: Thank you! I think I will.

 Father, Jake and Jesse had a seat.

Father: OK, folks I need for you to tell me everything.
 So you say you know that Satan is possessing you all and possibly your child too.

Chapter 7

The Wilson's (Jake and Jesse), begin to tell Father Milan what his father-in-law told him, why he was doing the things he was doing and he told his daughter- Jesse, why she was doing the things she was doing.
They (Jake and Jesse) told Father Milan about their killings and rituals about eating the parts of the victims in a stew they made when they got home.
They are really upset to have that curse on them and that's the reason that they got in touch with him to have this exorcism done, in order to live a normal life for them and their child.

Father: OK. I've heard enough. What I want you to do is don't tell anyone that I'm going to perform this exorcism.

Jake and Jesse: OK, we won't. (They responded together)

Father: OK, good. Tomorrow I'll be here at 9:00 am to perform the procedure.

Jake: Oh! Good, we'll be ready.

Jesse: That's for sure!

The next morning at 9:00 am the Priest arrived at their house. They said their Good mornings to each other and the Priest directed them to go into their bedroom.
He went into the other bedroom and came out in full garb with a sizeable cross, HOLY WATER and prayer (Blessed) cloth and proceed to the bedroom where they were (Jake and Jesse) waiting, sitting on the bed.
The Priest entered the room with the cross and prayer cloth in his left hand and HOLY WATER in his right.
As he was entering the room he was praying an exorcism prayer to get rid of the demons from out of Jake and Jesse

and the surrounding areas.

Priest: I'm saying this prayer in the name of OUR LORD GOD THROUGH HIS SON, JESUS CHRIST. If you're in there Satan, show yourself and erase yourself out of the lives of these two people. I'm here to send you back into the depths of hell where you belong.

At that moment, a hard wind with a loud spooky, evil and menacing sound with the wind coming from outside, opening the bedroom window with an unearthly evil force of strength into the room with Jake and Jesse on the bed.
With Jake and Jesse sitting on the bed, the wind pushed them and the bed against the wall. With the bed leaning straight up on the wall with Jake and Jesse still sitting on the bed in mid-air against gravity.
Their bodies transformed into a demon typed creature, the looks of it was so frightened, it startled and scared the Priest for a few seconds, but he stayed focused and kept on praying for the demon to get out of the couple's body, out of the room, out of this world and get back to the depths of hell where it belongs.

In the meantime the Priest was always holding the cross and prayer cloth in his left hand and extended straight out towards Jake and Jesse up close and personal, simultaneously back and forth to him and her with authority praying to get rid of the demons.
And in his right hand he was holding a bottle of HOLY WATER that when you squeeze it the water will squirt out.

Priest: I command you back to the depths of hell. Satan, I command you: IN THE NAME OF THE FATHER AND OF THE SON AND OF THE HOLY SPIRIT, right now from GOD THROUGH HIS LOVING SON JESUS CHRIST! Leave this place now.

At that time a hard wind came up from nowhere and caused the Priest to bend over, he started to squirt the HOLY WATER on Jake and Jesse. When the water touched their skin, it burned them and smoke was coming from their bodies.

The Priest kept giving a strong convicting prayer for the demon to leave and go back to hell where it belongs. The wind subsided, the Priest stood straight up again and started to squirt more water on Jake and Jesse, saying out loud: IN THE NAME OF THE FATHER AND OF THE SON AND OF THE HOLY SPIRIT, I command you Satan to leave these people and go back into the depths of hell where you belong.

Whenever he squirt the HOLY WATER on them, a much more prominent demonic evil sound comes out of the both of them. He squirted some more HOLY WATER on them, accompanied by the same but more gruesome evil demonic sound each time.

The Priest kept squirting the HOLY WATER on them and as he was looking at them hoping that the cross, HOLY WATER, prayer cloth (he was holding the prayer cloth in his left hand with the cross) and hoping that prayers would do the job to get rid of the demons, but at no avail.

The Priest was getting worried. At that time, a black greyish cloud was forming out of the bodies of Jake and Jesse. (The cloud formed into one entity, which came out of Jake and Jesse). It was very evil, it was very scary, but the Priest kept fighting it back repeatedly saying, be gone IN THE NAME OF THE FATHER AND OF THE SON AND OF THE HOLY SPIRIT, I command you Satan, to come out of these people and leave this place and go back to the depths of hell where you belong.

The demons formed itself fully looking of an evil formation that is not of this world. From out of nowhere - it – shot some iron stakes at the Priest, pinning him to the wall and seconds later, the demons shot some more stakes into the Priest's eyes and four long stakes (the stakes where just appearing out of thin air) went straight to the Priest's heart, killing him instantly. After the demons killed the priest, they left and immediately everything changed back somewhat peaceful.

When everything was said and done considering what all just happen, Jake and Jesse wasn't harm at all.

Jake and Jesse became back focused after the demons left there for the time being and they looked towards the Priest and saw what the demons had done to him.

They both almost simultaneously said:

Jake: Ooh LORD! (In a loud hysterical voice) What in the hell happen here.

Jesse screamed very loudly in hysterics, breathing in and out very hard.

Jake looked around, felt safe it was okay to leave. He grabbed Jesse by the hand and said to her:

Jake: Come on Jesse, let's get out of here.

Jesse: Unhuh!!!

Jake pulled her off the bed and began to get out of the house. She rose up, very confused, but proceeded to follow with his hand still holding hers very tightly, on their way out of the house.

When they got outside, Jake and Jesse went to their car and drove to the nearest public telephone and called the Catholic Church the Priest was working out of.

(Phone ringing)

Secretary at Church: Hello

Jake: Can I speak to the Priest on duty.

Secretary: Sure, who's calling?

Jake: Jake Wilson!

Secretary: Hold on, let me transfer you to him.

The Priest that's on duty answers!

Priest: Hello, Mr. Wilson, what can I help you with?

Jake: Sir your friend, Father Milan was performing an exorcism on myself and my wife but something went terribly wrong.

Priest: What happened wrong?

Jake: We woke up (him and wife) and Father Milan was pinned up against the wall full of spikes, dead. We must have blanked out in the middle of the exorcism. When we woke up there he was pinned dead on the wall with spikes all over his body.

Priest: Oh, my GOD have mercy. What's the address to your place? We have to get there immediately to get him.

Jake said: OK! And he (Jake) gave the Priest his address.

They arrived (The clergymen) at Jake and Jesse's house. They were sitting (Jake and Jesse) outside their house in their car waiting for them to get there. The clergymen (four of them) showed up. Jake and Jesse saw them drive up.

Jake: Stay here honey, let me go meet them and give them the keys.

Because Jake and Jesse didn't want to be nowhere around when they were there doing what they had to do!

Jesse: OK, I'm not moving.

Jake walked up to the clergymen's car. They were getting out of the car.
. Jake walked up towards them to meet them to give them the keys.
At that time the clergymen were getting out of the car, one by one
. Jake walked towards the driver of the automobile and asked him:

Jake: Hello, are you the Priest I spoke with on the phone (the other clergymen were out of the car just standing around). The driver said:

Driver Priest: Yes, I am. You must be Mr. Wilson.

Jake: Yes, I am. Well here are the keys.

Driver Priest: Oh! Thanks. Well we will take over from here.

Jake: OK.

Jake: We are not (Jake and Jesse) going to stay around, but we will be close by!

Father: OK! Good, we would have to do this ourselves anyway.

Jake: OK.

Jake: OK, I understand.

Driver Priest: When we're done we will give you guys a call, to come to our offices to discuss what's going on. Be safe.

Jake: OK, Sir Thanks, will talk to you later.

Jake and Jesse drove off to let the clergymen take care of their business.
They went and hung out at the beach, (Jake and Jesse) to somewhat help calm themselves down a bit.

The clergymen went into the house very carefully and cautiously. They entered into the living room. They all stayed together, looking around for anything out of the ordinary. So far so good until they got into the bedroom and there was their fellow clergyman pinned up against the wall dead with spikes stuck in him all over his body.

They looked and immediately one of them started praying, saying, OUR FATHER IN THE NAME OF YOUR SON JESUS CHRIST, if there is a presence of a demonic, evil spirit still in here, through your love, your grace and in the blood of your loving SON JESUS CHRIST, let it be gone forever and Our Gracious FATHER, take it and send it where it belongs and that's into the depths of hell forever.
We ask and pray for these blessings through your loving and gracious SON JESUS CHRIST, OUR LORD and we thank you for all these many blessings MY LORD GOD, AMEN.

They stood and watched for a while until they were comfortable enough to proceed to unstake their fellow clergymen off of the wall.
They proceeded to do just that.
After they got him down, one of the clergymen called the Church to send the Church Van.
They gave the driver of the Van (caretaker of the Church) the address with all the information, of what they needed the Van for.
The driver responded saying, MY LORD OK! I'll be there

shortly.

A little while later the caretaker arrived at the house of the Wilson's, where the deceased Father was.

One of the clergymen was standing on the front porch waiting for him.

Caretaker: Hello Sir. What do you need me to do?

Father: Come on inside and I'll show you.

They both walked in where the deceased Priest was in the bedroom. They all had to get together to pick him up and put him in a body bag and transport him into the Van and bring him to the church.

In the meantime, while they were in the process of moving the body of their fellow clergyman, other than the caretaker, each Priest was saying continually special prayers of comfort, protection, healing, and repentance, as they were carrying the body out of the house to the Van.

They successfully got the Father body to the church, placed it down in a secret corridor in the basement of the church. Where they kept him until one of the Fathers could get in touch with the Vatican to let them know what happened to the Priest and what would be the next step to do, concerning what to do with the body of the Priest.

And what to do about the married couple, Jake and Jesse (Mr. and Mrs. Wilson) whom the exorcism was performed on that led to the death of the Priest by the evil and demonic spirits which is possessing them.

They got in touch with the Vatican and a Cardinal close to the Pope relayed a message to the fellow clergymen of the deceased Priest that from the information that they gave to them about how everything that transpired during the exorcism and the way that the clergyman died.

That what they were dealing with is a higher statue demonic spirit of rank in Satan's world of terror.

First that they would not relay what happened to nobody.

The reason for that is because we don't want to jeopardize no one else or allowing them to be vulnerable to the demonic curse that's possessing the married couple (Mr. and Mrs. Wilson).

Afterwards burn the body of the slain Priest and make sure his ashes blow into the atmosphere towards the east when it is a very windy day.

The Pope and his close advisors are going to appoint a highly reputable Apostle, who can eradicate the demons out of the married couple and perform a special exorcism to capture and send the demonic spirit entity back and straight to the depths of hell, to where it belongs from here to eternity.

Cardinal: Sir, I'll call you in a few days to let you know when the Apostle will reach your town and where he will be staying.

Priest #3: OK, sounds good.

Cardinal: When he gets there he'll give you a call, should he ask for you.

Priest #3: Yes, that'll be fine.

Cardinal: OK, what's your name? I'll relay it to him (Apostle) who to ask for.

Priest #3: I'm, Father William. He can call this same number and ask for me.
I will be close by.

Cardinal: OK, good. Talk to you later.

Priest #3: OK, goodbye.

Cardinal: Bye.

They hung up the phones, saying their goodbyes.

Chapter 8

A day later the Apostle called the Catholic Church.

Phone ringing:

Father William: Hello!

Apostle: Hello, yes may I speak to Father William?

Father William: Yes, this is me. Who is it?

Apostle: This is Apostle Job, I'm in town at the Holiday Inn on Colorado and Ocean Avenue, Room 204. Can you come and get me?

Father William: Yes I can. Let me get things situated here and I'll be there within the hour.

Apostle: OK! Good. Look forward to meeting you.

Father William: Same here, see you soon. Bye.

Apostle: OK, bye.

Father William arrived at the Holiday Inn, parked in the hotel parking lot, walked to the front desk and requested to call and let Apostle Job know that he (Father William) is downstairs waiting on him.
The desk clerk called Apostle Job to let him know that Father William was in the lobby area, waiting on him to come down.

Apostle Job- talking to desk clerk.

Apostle Job: Uh, Sir tell and direct Father William to come on up to my room. I'll be waiting for him up here, so we can sit and chat for a while.

Desk Clerk: OK Sir, will do.

Desk Clerk: Sir, Apostle Job wants you to come up to his room.

Father William: OK, how do I get there?

Desk Clerk: Go straight, make a right to the elevator go up to second floor. When you get out of the elevator make a left, go straight down maybe 5 or 6 doors to Room 204. It'll be on the right side of the corridor.

Father William: OK! I got it. Thanks very much.

Desk Clerk: You're welcome.

 Father William proceeded to go to Apostle Job room.
 He arrived at the Apostle Job door, knocked on the door.
The door opened and Apostle Job greeted him by saying:

Apostle: Hi Father William, come on in.

Father William: OK, thank you.

Apostle: Have a seat.

Father William: I think I will have a seat.

Father William sat in the chair next to the TV.
 Apostle Job sat on the bed.

Apostle: How've you been?

Father William: I've been good, being disciplined, obedient and keeping the faith for GOD THROUGH HIS SON JESUS CHRIST.

Apostle: I agree. I understand. So tell me about the situation at hand.

Father William: Well, it's a married couple and on the wife's side of the family. Well they are devil worshippers. The husband married into the family not knowing who they are. Satan got them pregnant with his (Satan's) child. They both are possessed, but the husband wants the demons out of their bodies and life, and so does his wife.

Apostle: OK, I've heard of this kind of situation before. I look forward to meeting with them (husband and wife, Jake and Jesse).

Father William: OK, when do you want me to set it up, for you all to meet?

Apostle: Call them today and let them know that I want to meet with them tomorrow around 10:00 am, if that's a good time for them.

Father William: OK, will do.

Apostle: Father come pick me up at 8:00 am. By that time we can go to IHOP and have breakfast before we meet with Mr. and Mrs. Wilson, if things go as planned.

Father William: OK! Will do.

Father William proceeded to leave.

They said their goodbyes and Father assured that he will relay the message and will be there at 8:00 am to pick him (Apostle) up, if that schedule was good for the Wilsons (Jake and Jesse).
Father William called the married couple (Jake and Jesse)

and explained to them that himself and Apostle Job will meet with them tomorrow at their home around 10:00 am and would that be a good time for them.

Jake answered the phone and he said, yes!

That time is good.

Father William emphasized to them to take it easy and be safe.

Jake replied: Will do.

They said their goodbyes and hung up the phones.

The next morning, everybody met up at Jake and Jesse's home.

By the way Father William and Apostle Job had breakfast at the IHop restaurant that morning, before heading towards the Wilsons's house.

They all were sitting down inside the house.

Father William, Apostle Job, Jake and Jesse in Jake and Jesse's living room.

Apostle Job started to begin discussing and layout of the plan, how they will proceed to perform the exorcism.

He concluded that it must happen in an open area far away from people and he suggested that the best place for that, would be somewhere in the high mountains like the San Bernardino Mountains in a very remote and isolated area.

They all agreed.

They agreed to meet at the Wilson's house, the next morning.

Father William picked up Apostle Job at the hotel the next morning.

They drove to the Wilson's, Father William parked the Van on the street in front of the Wilsons house.

They both got out and they both walked up to the Wilsons door.

Father William knocked on the door. Jesse answered the door.

Jesse: Hi, come on in Sirs.

Father William and Apostle Job: OK! Thanks (speaking simultaneously)

Jake was coming from out of their bedroom into the living room.
He acknowledged Father William, Apostle Job and Jesse standing in the living room.
He responded by saying:

Jake: Please, have a seat you all.

They did, including Jesse.

Jake: How is everything?

Father William: Everything is okay.

Apostle Job: I'm doing great.

Jesse is just observing and listening to the conversation.

Father William: Are you guys prepared for our rendezvous today in the hills?

Jake and Jesse: Yes, we are (speaking simultaneously).

Apostle Job: How long will it take for you guys to be ready to leave, so we can be on our way to get to where we have to go?

Jake: Give us 30 minutes. In the meantime, would you all like to have anything?

Father William: Uh! Yes, I'd like some coffee.

Apostle Job: I'll take some hot tea.

Jake: Jesse, can you get that for them please honey? While I get our gear together?

Jesse: OK, will do.

Jesse went into the kitchen to fix drinks for the clergymen and returned and said:

Jesse: Tea for you Apostle Job, coffee for you Father William.

She gave tea to Apostle Job and coffee to Father William.

Apostle Job: Thank you very much.

Father William: Thank you very much.

 They sat and watch TV while drinking their drinks.
 Jesse went into the bedroom to help Jake get everything together for the rendezvous.

Time passed!

 The clergymen finished their drinks and about that time the Wilsons came out of the bedroom, ready to go.
 They all (the clergymen, the Wilsons) each grabbed a piece of gear and equipment and headed outside towards the SUV to pack everything in the Van.
 They are using the transportation from Father William Church! The clergymen gear and equipment were already in the Van. Father William was driving and asked was everybody ready and okay?

They all answered yes.

They secured everything in the SUV.

They all got in the Van and drove off towards their destination.
On the way everything was quiet because Father William put on a sermon on the radio for them all to listen to as they were traveling.
They got to their destination!
It was still morning.

Father William: We're here! Everybody's fine?

They all said yes, we're okay!
They got out of the Van, taking out what they had to have to set up camp.
They parked in the designated areas for campers.

Father William: Well, does anybody have any suggestions which way we should start to walk, to find a good camp site?

Apostle Job: Yes, let's travel heading north.

Father William had a compass he looked on it and said north is straight ahead.
They started walking.
They walked about a mile and found a very desirable camping spot.
They decided to camp there.
Jake and Jesse set up their tent.
Father William set up his tent and Apostle Job set up his.
After they set their tents up they all sat around a campfire, roasting marshmallows and drinking hot chocolate.
They had a conversation about everything until they all got tired.
Father Williams put out the camp fire and they all, went into their tents
They were either reading their Bible, listening to iPod or just relaxing or watching battery operated television, eating food and snacks, periodically before they retired for the night.

Father William went to the Jake and Jesse's tent to say have a good night, then to Apostle Job to say to him to have a good night also.

They all fell asleep around 1 or 2 am in the morning.

Father William, Jesse and Apostle Job, woke up to a very terrifying noise around 5am in the morning.

Father William exited his tent.

Apostle Job exited his tent.

They looked at each other.

At that time Jesse came out of her and her husband Jake tent very hysterical and scared and saw the Father and the Apostle standing side by side and said to them, Jake is being possessed.

Apostle Job said: Okay! One minute, be right back.

He went into his tent and retrieved a sizeable cross, which he had in his

Tent just for this purpose and HOLY WATER, put on a robe, got the large cross to hold in his hand a black scarf to go around his neck.

He went to Jesse and Jake's tent, walked in and there was Jake lying down on his back, arms stretched out over his head, legs and feet pointed stiff and his skin was a bright orange color. His body was levitating in mid-air.

Apostle Job took out his HOLY WATER and sprinkled some on Jake, saying:

Apostle Job: IN THE NAME OF OUR L0RD GOD THROUGH HIS SON JESUS CHRIST I command you to come out of this man and leave and go back into the depths of hell where you belong, Satan!

The devil in the possessed man answered in a very evil, loud and demonic voice saying if or when I do leave, you and him

is coming with me.
At that time a ball of fire came from the possessed man's hand, knocked the tent into the air into the woods.
 The Apostle Job kept repeating the same phrase when the fire came out.
 The Apostle backed up a little but kept his ground.
 At that time the possessed man was levitating in mid air, straight up and went demonic powers started throwing things that was lying around on the forest floor, just by thinking of it and was trying to burn the Apostle Job also.
 But none of it was effective because Apostle Job did his homework on the demon he was encountering.
The demon possessed man said in a very loud and demonic voice saying I am a high Priest from Satan himself.
 I'm here to kill and take your soul with me to torture forever and ever - haaaaaaaa - I will kill - haaaaaaaaaa.
At that time, Apostle Job started Praying!

Apostle Job: OUR FATHER WHO ART IN HEAVEN, MY GOD THROUGH HIS SON JESUS CHRIST, I command you to leave this man and return to the depths of hell where you belong, forever and ever in the name of OUR LORD GOD THROUGH HIS SON JESUS CHRIST. I command this demon to leave now.

 The demon in the man created and erupted, demons with horns and pitch forks to pop up out of the ground to attack the Apostle.
 At that time the Apostle told Father William and Jesse to run fast and keep running until they got out of there.

 They did, (Father William and Jesse) as Apostle Job suggested.

 As the demons were popping up out of the ground, the Apostle Job stood his ground and one by one was dissolving them by repeating his prayer with conviction and sprinkling

them with HOLY WATER and showing them the cross.
But they kept on coming and the Apostle kept getting rid of them.
And then things got quiet for a minute.
Possessed man, (Jake) was still in mid-air.
And all of a sudden the earth started to open wide, fire and smoke coming from out of it and from out of the earth was a very ferocious and evil demonic sound.
And appeared was Satan himself.
The Apostle Job stood his ground.
Satan gave out a ferocious sounding voice against the Apostle and at that time, Apostle Job said out loud:

MY LORD GOD IN THE NAME OF JESUS CHRIST and at that instant a voice from above very loud and with strong conviction said:

"I AM THE LORD THY GOD. I AM THE ALPHA, I AM THE OMEGA, I AM THE CREATOR OF ALL THINGS. Satan I command you to leave this place and go back to the depths of hell where you belong."

The Apostle put his head down when THE LORD showed his presence as a bright cloud.

Satan looked at the bright cloud of the LORD'S and in an instant immediately disappeared.

THE LORD'S VOICE came out of the bright cloud, told Apostle Job good work my good and faithful servant.

Go in peace!

The bright cloud of THE LORD disappeared and Jake returned back lying on the ground.

Apostle Job looked up and saw that the bright cloud of THE

LORD GOD was gone and at that time Jake woke up, asking what happened.

Apostle: Wow! Man you were possessed by the devil. It was very scary. I had to send your wife and Father William away for their safety.

Jake: How long have I been out of it?

Apostle: Close to 45 minutes. How do you feel?

Jake: I don't feel bad, just a little sluggish.

Apostle: THE SPIRIT OF THE LORD GOD, appeared to help me out.

Jake: Really. Whoa! Really.

Apostle: Yes, let's get out of here. I'll tell you about everything that went on, but let's get back to Father William and your wife.

Jake: OK!

 They headed on back towards where Father William and his wife was, but on the way Apostle was filling him on what happened when he was possessed.
 It was a bunch of ooohs and aaahhhs, and whoaaas and wows from Jake, the whole time Apostle was telling him what happened.
They (Apostle and Jake) kept their bearings together and kept on traveling out of the camp site, to where they were (Father William and Jesse).
After a while they arrived where Father William and Jake wife are.
When they became close enough to see them in eyesight, Father William was looking in the rear view mirror

occasionally.

When he saw Apostle Job and Jake walking up, he said to Jake's wife there they are!

Jake wife said who?

Father William said them, Apostle Job and Jake.

She turned around, looking through the back window and saw them walking up.

She opened up the door and Father Williams did the same thing (opened up the door), but she got out first and started running towards her husband.

At the same time he, (Jake) spotted her and started to run towards her.

Father William was walking fast right behind her (Jake's wife) and Apostle Job was walking fast behind Jake, heading towards Father William to meet and to know if everything has been alright and to tell him what happened and the outcome of the situation that they were in.

Jesse and Jake met one another and started to give one another a lot of hugs and kisses.

Jesse: Is everything okay?

Jake: Yes, are you alright?

Jesse: Yes I am. What happened back there?

Jake: Apostle Job will let you know what happened. He explained it to me already.

And right after they met Father William and Apostle Job! They gave each other a manly hug and asked one another was everything alright.

Father William: Yes, everything was okay out here.

Apostle Job: Everything went well with the exorcism.

Father William: Did you get rid of the demons?

Apostle Job: Yes we did. Let's get in the Van and get out of here and I'll tell you everything that went on.

Father William: Okay.

 They all got in the Van they all exchanged pleasant greetings to one another.
 Apostle Job, began to tell Jesse and Father William what went down back at the camp site while performing the exorcism.

Apostle Job: Uh! Guys it got rough back there. Jake was going through some very peculiar and dangerous situations, but I stayed the course to work to keep it at a minimum, hoping that the situation wouldn't get any worse.
Demons were popping up everywhere and I was killing them, but it started to get out of hand and Satan himself showed up.
 His appearance was that of some type of animal, the looks was like nothing in this world.
 He was about 3 ½ feet tall, two small pointed horns on top of his head, long pointed hands with long nails, pointed nose, a tail that was proportioned with his body and the end of his tail was shaped like a spear, his feet was like the hoofs of a goat, and his eyes was fire red just like his whole body, he was without sex organs, and he had a pitch fork in his hand with three prongs, at the end they were shaped like an arrow.

I was getting prepared to fight him, but THE SRIRIT OF THE LORD GOD showed up, it was a bright cloud came from the sky and hovered over us, and a very deep voice came out of it saying,

I AM THE LORD THY GOD. I AM THE ALPHA, I AM THE OMEGA. I AM THE CREATOR OF ALL THINGS. Satan, I commanded you to leave this place and go straight back to the depths of hell where you belong.

And Satan and his demons obeyed GOD's command. They disappeared immediately!

They all (Jake, Father William and Jesse were in an incredible display of ahhhs, ooohs, ooooohs, and wow's to the story, Apostle Job had just told them.
 On their way there after Apostle Job got finish telling everybody about what happened while he was performing the exorcism, they chilled for a while (not talking), still in route to Jake and Jesse's house.

 After a little time had passed (still riding in the Van), Apostle Job replied by saying I can go for some food now, everybody else agreed.
 So they arrived at Jake and Jesse's house, while at the house Jesse went into the kitchen and started to fix dinner for everybody.

In the meantime, Father William, Apostle Job and Jake was just having a casual conversation sitting in the living room.

Apostle Job: Uh, Jake, how are you feeling?

Jake: I'm feeling great. Just a little hungry.

Father William: Yes, I can eat something too.

Apostle Job: Isn't your wife cooking something in the kitchen?

Jake: Yes, she's good at whipping something up fast and good. We should be eating soon.

Apostle Job and Father William: OK! Good.

Apostle Job: I need to call the Pope and relay to him the

outcome of the exorcism.

Jake: OK Sir, you can use our landline if you wish.

Apostle Job: OK, I think I will. It would be appreciated.

Jake: There it is (Jake pointing to where the phone is), on the dresser in the hallway.

Apostle Job: OK, thanks.

Apostle Job walked over to the phone, sat in the chair next to the phone and called the Pope.
(Apostle Job has a direct phone number to the Pope's Office)

Apostle Job: (phone ringing) May I speak to Pope Timothy?

Party on other end: Who's calling?

Apostle Job: This is Apostle Job.

Party on other end: Hold on one second.

Apostle Job: OK, I will.

Party on other end: Apostle Job?

Apostle Job: Yes.

Party on other end: Hold on one second. I'm going to transfer you to Pope Timothy, right now.

Apostle Job: Okay, Thanks.

The Pope: Hello! Apostle Job.

Apostle Job: Hello Sir, how are you?

The Pope: I'm well. How did things go with the exorcism?

Apostle Job: Well Sir! Maybe about 1 or 2 in the morning we all were in our tents asleep and a loud demonic sound came from out of the Wilson's tent.
That's Mr. and Mrs. Jake and Jesse Wilson!
 Mr. Jake was possessed.
 We went right to work myself and Father William, but it got out of hand with the demons.
 At that point, I told Father William to get out of here and take Mrs. Wilson with him and go back to where the Van was.

 They did!

 I started to perform the procedures myself, I had control for a while, but as time went on it started to get out of hand and a miracle happened.

The SPIRIT OF THE LORD GOD showed up in a bright cloud, came and rescued us out of the situation and the Voice of GOD(came from out of the cloud) commanded the devil Satan himself and his demons to leave this place and go back to the depths of hell where they belong.

Satan and his demons!
 Complied with GOD'S commands and immediately disappeared.
 Back to hell where they belong!

The Pope: PRAISE THE LORD! What myself and the Cardinals, will do here is to go into collaboration of a series of special prayer's to communicate with OUR LORD GOD THROUGH HIS SON JESUS CHRIST and see how long we can keep him and his demons there.
 Maybe OUR LORD GOD will bless us to have the wisdom and power to keep him (Satan) and his demons down in the

depths of hell forever.

Chapter 9

Apostle Job: OK, Sir, I will pray my prayers also for the same thing.

Pope Timothy: OK, good. When will you be back to the Vatican?

Apostle Job: I'm going to stay here for three more days, just to monitor things to make sure everything is alright.

Pope Timothy: OK, good. Have a blessed and safe trip back. When you get here, come and meet with me so that we can go over things.

Apostle Job: OK Sir, will do. I will talk to you later.

Pope Timothy: OK, good. See and talk to you then.

Apostle Job: OK, bye Sir.

Pope Timothy: OK, bye.

They hung up the phone with goodbyes to one another!

Apostle Job went back into the living room where everybody was, when he got off the phone talking to the Pope.
Jake's wife Jesse was out of the kitchen socializing, while the food was still cooking.
He entered (Apostle Job) the living room, saying I see everybody's here.
Hello everybody!
In unison, they all said hello back.

Apostle Job: I talked to Pope Timothy. Everything's okay. I'll be heading back to the Vatican in three days.

Father William: OK, sounds good. How is the Pope?

Apostle Job: He's well.

Father William: Apostle Job, tell the Pope I said hello and wish him well when you get back.

Apostle Job: Will do. Uh! Jake or Jesse, would you like to send a message to Pope Timothy?

Jake: Yes, I would!

Jesse: I would also!

Jake: Tell him I love him and thank him for his support and blessings through our times of troubles.

Jesse: Tell him I love him also and to keep up in his prayers, and GOD bless him for giving us his support through our times of troubles.

Apostle Job: OK, will do.

It was a quiet moment!
Everybody calmed down without conversation and just started to check the news out that was on the television at that time. Jesse said that she was going to check on the food. Everybody said okay.

Jake: Sounds good. I know that we all are ready to eat.

Everybody agreed!

Jesse got up and went into the kitchen to check on the food. At that time a special bulletin came on TV on the news. They were watching that our President (of the United States of America) will be having a special news conference at 8:00

pm tonight.

They all agreed no matter what they were doing at that time, they were going to watch and see what he have to say.

At that time, Jesse came out of the kitchen and announced that dinner is served.

Everybody had their individual comments saying oh yea! Yes! Alright!

They proceeded to go to the dining area and they all took a seat at the dining area table.

Jesse had already set the table with plates, etc. before she went into the kitchen to start cooking.

They ate, afterwards relaxed and watched a little television before Father William and Apostle Job decided to leave and head on back to where they were residing.

The all was giving well wishes, blessings and goodbyes.

Afterwards Father William and Apostle Job left.

Father William dropped the Apostle off at his Hotel room. Apostle Job went to his Hotel room, read a few scriptures out of his Bible, and then retired and went to bed for the night. Father William went back to the seminary, consulted with superiors about what happened and then he retired (went to sleep) for the night.

That night, they all were so tired they forgot all about the President's speech, they were supposed to watch.

The next morning Apostle Job called the Vatican and informed them that he would be leaving for Vatican City today.

He said (Apostle Job) that he's leaving early because he feels that everything is fine.

His flight leaves this afternoon at 3:00 pm and he will call them to come and pick him up when he arrives at the airport.

Father William, returned to work in the Parish at the Church as Priest.

And Jake and Jesse went back to their profession.

They (Jake and Jesse) woke up the next morning, had breakfast and they got themselves together to go to work. When they got there at work everything seemed normal as usual.

But little did they know that while they were having the exorcism performed on him the SPIRIT OF THE LORD, with his divine powers eradicated all the demons who were possessing Jake and Jesse and everyone who is close to them.

GOD casted all the demons straight down into the depths of hell at the command of OUR FATHER, THE LORD GOD.

Business went on as usual, but stealing, killing and trying to create dominion over certain things that they are interested in for evil purposes ceased.
They all are unaware, except Jake and Jesse that they all are working their business for THE LORD and themselves and there is no hanky panky or evil doings, period!

As time went on, Jake and Jesse worked until Jesse had to take a maternity leave.
She gave birth to a son, they named him, Jhikiva.
(P.S.) the name Jhikiva means the chosen one!
Life was good for the Wilson's.
They would spend a lot of time at the in-laws and with family and friends.
Jake and Jesse always kept in touch with Father William and Apostle Job, periodically to always check to see how each other is doing.
The parents of Jesse were never told about the exorcism.
The parents of Jesse was affected by the exorcism!

THE HOLY SPIRIT OF THE LORD GOD entered into them and changed their way of thinking and living, and now they were working for THE LORD GOD, Through HIS SON JESUS

CHRIST.

The parent's organization prospered in good tidings, focusing on creating jobs and serving the people in the name of THE LORD.
They didn't have a clue that their lives (Jesse's parents) had been transformed into living with the will of GOD in them to carry out his work (THE LORD GOD).
As time went by, the Vatican spokespersons and the Pope himself to everyone involved to always pray the prayer that the Pope instructed them.
How to pray to keep the devil at bay, and into the depths of hell for the next 1000 years.

Time went on everybody involved in the exorcism was living a comfortable and peaceful life.
Jake and Jesse were still working at their jobs.
Jesse was on maternity leave for a year.
When she started back working, she would leave about an hour earlier from her job before Jake.

(This was their job hours) in order for her, to pick up the baby from her Mother's house (Her mother volunteered to babysit her grandson). So she and the baby can be at home before Jake knocks off from work.

Jake: (He arrived home, opened the door and said) Honey, I'm home, where are you?

Jesse: (She heard him and responded) I'm in the kitchen.

He walked into the kitchen where she was and said:

Jake: Honey, how is the baby?

Jesse: He's good he's sleep in his bassinet in the bedroom.

Jake: OK, good Honey. I got promoted at the job to CEO of the company and the pay is both of ours combined and a lot more! You don't have to work anymore.

Jesse: Ooohhh great! That means that I can stay home and raise Jhikiva?

Jake: Exactly! Isn't that a great blessing, Praise the Lord!

Jesse: Yes it is, Praise the Lord.

They were so happy about the good news, they could hardly compose themselves to get relaxed. But they calm down and the blessing was entering into their lives from that day forward and forever.
 The next morning Jake went back to his workplace with a new job title (CEO) of the company.
When he got there he was greeted very warmly and respectful.
His personal secretary Mrs. Jamison was there waiting to escort him after he was greeted to his new position.
His secretary introduced herself to him and informed him of some of his basic duties and to show him his new office.
They arrived at his new office himself and Mrs. Jamison.

Mrs. Jamison: Well here we are!

Mrs. Jamison gave him the master key to his office door and every door in the building.
 There was his name and title on the door! Mr. Jake Wilson, CEO.
Jake accepted the key and took a look at the door.

Jake: Wow, this is nice. I know I am going to love this.

Mrs. Jamison: That's good. I know you will too, Mr. Wilson.

Jake: Well, let's go in. (He opened the door and they walked in the office).

Mrs. Jamison knew the setup in the office, but everything was new to Jake.

Jake: Wow, this is nice. (There was a computer, huge fish tank with exotic fish, big screen TV in the lounge and a mini kitchen).
To tell you the truth it had just about everything and even a very spacious patio.

Mrs. Jamison: I knew you would love it.

Jake: Yes, I really do. I am ecstatic! THANK GOD THROUGH HIS SON JESUS CHRIST, for everything!

Mrs. Jamison: Amen, Sir. I am happy that you have found everything is in order. I have to get back to work. If you need me for anything just call me on the intercom system on the desk. It's linked directly to me.

Jake: OK, great. Thanks for everything. Have a good day.

Mrs. Jamison: You are welcome, will do, and talk to you later. You have a good day too, Sir.

Jake: OK, Thanks! I will.

Mrs. Jamison walked to the door and asked Jake if he wanted the door closed.
He said yes and she closed the door.

Jake kicked back in his chair at his desk (thinking to himself) to check all departments they have in the firm and to call and talk on the intercom system to his secretary, to let everybody know that he wants to have a meeting to introduce himself to everyone and to speak to them to advise them what kind of program of operation he has in mind to maintain the company to keep running smoothly, successful and very profitable.

 Plus have feedback from employees about suggestions from them that they can input some ideas to keep the company successful and profitable.

 That we can decide whether or not if it's conducive for the company's growth or not.

 So he did (call secretary) and they set up a meeting for the following Friday at the end of the workweek.

After Jake talked to the secretary and to set up the meetings with employees he retired for the day and proceeded to go home to his family.

 He went to his car in the parking garage, in his personal parking place for the CEO of the company. Got into his leased company Ferrari, and drove home taking the same route he was taking when he was just a worker.

 And now he's CEO of the company, he's driving the same route to and from home.

When he arrived home, he parked his car in the car space in front of the garage.

By the way Jesse knew about the Ferrari, she loved it!

 Jesse (his wife) heard him pull up and decided that when he opened the front door to come in, she is going to be behind the door to surprise him, just to see what kind of
Reaction she can get out of him (just for play).

 He opened the door, and called for his wife.

Jake: Jesse, where are you?

Before he can say anything else, Jesse came from behind the door and said:

Jesse: Boo! (Real loud)

Jake: Whoa! (In a very shocked and surprised voice.)

They looked at one another and started laughing aloud with a very wholesome spirited laugh and embraced one another with a passionate hug and kiss.

Jake: That was funny. It kind of scared me a little. I was relieved that it was you.

Jesse: Ha! Ha! Ha! You had a very peculiar look on your face. Ha! Ha! Ha!

Jake: OK, don't rub it in the ground.

Jesse: OK, how was your day honey?

(Jesse is still giggling a little)

Jake: It was great! The new office is immaculate and I have a real nice and respectful secretary and the both of us set up a meeting, so that I can meet and speak with all of the staff.

Jesse: Oh! Good. That's great!

He locked the door and they proceeded to walk to the kitchen.

Jake: Where is Jhikiva?

Jesse: He's in his bedroom sleep.

Jake: I'll be back. I'm going to peek in on him.

Jesse: OK.

Jake went to his son's room, peaked in on him and indeed he was sleep.
He just stood and looked at his son for a while, feeling very

blessed and in his mind:
THANKING GOD THROUGH HIS SON JESUS for blessing
them with such a healthy and beautiful baby.
 When he was done admiring his son he proceeded to go back
to the kitchen where his wife was preparing dinner.

Jake: Baby! You know we are really blessed.

Jesse: Yes! You are absolutely right.

Jake: You know when we are really able we should start
giving back to people and to different charities we care about.

Jesse: I agree. I'm on board.

Jake: When we get a chance we're going to make a list of who
and what charities we're going to help.

Jesse: OK, sounds good to me!

 Jake had in mind before the conversation started what
charities he wanted to help and about what they are going to
do.

Jake: What's for dinner?

Jesse: Spaghetti and meatballs, potato salad and spinach with
dinner rolls.

Jake: Whoa, that sounds real good Honey. I know it's going to
taste just as good.

Jesse: Ooh! Thank you Baby!

Jake: You're welcome. What time will it be ready?

Jesse: In about another 15 minutes.

Jake: OK, good. Sometime before the week is over, we're gonna figure out who we're going to help. I have some ideas.

Jesse: OK, sounds good.

Jake went into the living room and sat in his reclining chair, turned on the TV and started to read the daily newspaper.
 Before long Jesse called Jake to let him know that dinner is ready.
 So they ate! After eating, Jake went back in the living room and watched TV.
 A little while later, Jesse came in after she finished, cleaning up the kitchen.
They watched TV together for a while and later that night retired and went to bed.
That whole week Jake and Jesse's routine was just about the same.
 For Jake it was going to work, taking the same route to work and back home.
 Same business at work as usual and same routine he does when he gets home,   playing with his son if he's not asleep.
 Talk to wife, eat dinner, watch TV and then retire for bed.
Jesse, same routine!
Fix breakfast for Jake, before he go to work and for son if he's up and not still asleep, doing regular housewife duties on occasion, go out to stores for different things for the house.
 Occasionally going out to different places her and her son just to get out of the house to enjoy the outdoors.

At the end of the week which was Friday, Jake before leaving home Jesse would walk him to the door if his son is awake.
 She would be holding him (her son).
 Jake would give them both a kiss and Jesse would say to him to have a good day honey and Jake would say OK, thanks sweetheart and you do too.
 And sometimes the baby would say something in baby talk

like sgree, gree, beelee to his daddy.
 He would kiss his son and say I love you and kiss his wife
and say I love you.
 And say to his wife to have a good day.
 Then he would walk out the door to his car and his wife and
son would be standing in the door until he drives off.
 When he drives off he blows the horn once and waves.
 And his wife would wave back and hold up their son's hand so
he can gesture a wave back too.

 Now he's on his way to work for his staff meeting.
He made it to the office and right away, business as usual.
That Friday (about one hour before punch out time for
employees) he had all his employees meet in the conference
room, where he had their general meetings for all staff.
They all assembled in the conference room, mingling amongst
one another, chit-chatting, enjoying refreshments until the
boss made his grand appearance.
 After maybe a half an hour lapsed!
 Jake walked into the conference room at 3:30 pm on that
Friday. As a matter of fact it was also payday for everybody.
Jake walked up to the podium and addressed the crowd.

Jake: Hello! Everybody.

Employees: Hello! Mr. Wilson.

Jake: How is everybody?

Employees: They all said different things like OK, good, great,
etc. but most of all they were all doing great.

Jake: I am your new boss. I'm very happy to be on board to
run our company. Some of the ones who were working before
the change and are still here after the new leadership, well
they know me because I was one of them.

For the new employees and the old, if there's any concerns about anything my doors are always open.

Jake proceeded to talk to the staff about the program he has in mind to keep the Corporation being very successful, prosperous, and helpful for everybody concerned.

When he was done with the speech at the meeting, the staff accepted him very favorably to lead their Corporation into the future.

After meeting, everybody mingled, talking to one another and expressing their pleasures to Mr. Wilson for having him as their boss.

After everything was over, everyone disbursed in an orderly fashion, doing different things such as taking doggy bags of food leftover, leaving together as carpool and different other scenarios people do after a staff meeting.

When everything was said and done, Jake left and went home, the usual way as always.

He arrived home doing the same routine as usual, went to open his door to his house, which his wife was there waiting for him behind the door.

He called out her name as usual and she would come out from behind the door on every occasion she does that.

She would say a different weird sounding word or sound to startle or try to scare him, only out of fun.

This day their son was up sitting in his high chair.

Jake started talking to him, asking him how he's doing.

I love you, come here then he picks him up out of his high chair and was holding him, talking, kissing and walking around with him just having fun, while Jesse gets dinner prepared for them.

They're at the dinner table (Father, Mother, and Son).

Jake blessed the food! They started eating.

Jake told Jesse what went on at the meeting this afternoon.

HIs son was just eating and looking and listening at his parent's conversation.

The relationship between the three (Father, Mother, Son) is very good and very blessed.

As for any type of demonic activities in their lives it was seized completely after the exorcism because, GOD has rebuked the devil and his demons and cast them down in the depths of hell for a 1,000 years before he (GOD) will let him out to roam around back here on Earth.

As for Jake and Jesse, and their son and everybody in their family and friends, fellow coworkers and any and everybody associated with them, was living a very blessed, successful and prosperous life.

 PRAISE THE LORD OUR GOD, THROUGH HIS SON JESUS CHRIST, MY LORD, AMEN.

      This Book Is Dedicated To My BEST FRIEND SONDRA LORETTA DIXON

My Love Always,

Nathaniel

Made in the USA
San Bernardino, CA
09 February 2016